MW01094144

Published by Backyard Studio Publishing
Harris, Minnesota (United States of America)

Publisher's Note: This is a work of fiction. Names, characters, places, and incidents are a product of the author's imagination. Locales and public names are sometimes used for atmospheric purposes. Any resemblance to actual people, living or dead, or to businesses, companies, events, institutions, or locales is completely coincidental. Although some real-life iconic places are depicted in settings, all situations and people related to those places are fictional.

Book Layout © 2017 BookDesignTemplates.com
Book Editing and Formatting by JeanneFelfe.com

Publisher's Cataloging-in-Publication Data
Names: Schultz, Esther, 1978-.
Title: What lies across the sea / Esther Schultz.
Description: Harris, MN : Backyard Studio Publishing, 2021. |
    Summary: A young woman visits her ancestral home in Italy for
    the first time, to fulfill the dying wishes of her mother. She
    discovers secrets of her mother's past and while facing adversity
    trying to unravel these secrets, discovers her own path in life.
Identifiers: LCCN 2021922346 | ISBN 9781737908616 (pbk.) | ISBN
    9781737908609 (ebook)
Subjects: LCSH: Family secrets -- Fiction. | Mothers and daughters --
    Fiction. | Self-actualization (Psychology) -- Fiction. |Women --
    Fiction. | Italy -- Fiction. | BISAC: FICTION / General. | FICTION
    / Women.
Classification: LCC PS3619.C48 W43 2021 (print) | PS3619.C48 (ebook) |
    DDC 813 S38—dc23
LC record available at https://lccn.loc.gov/ 2021922346

For Barb, who read my very first rough draft and told me to run with this thing called publishing a book.

And for Bri, who has been my biggest cheerleader. I love you more than you can say, stinker.

And also, for Rod, who supports me and all of my dreams with unfailing love.

Chapter One

The dust rose quickly and billowed in small clouds around Sarina Forester with each pedal forward on her well-used yellow bicycle toward town. It was a small town much like many in the Midwest, with small shops that lined its main street and churches that rose from various street corners. It had the normal small restaurants, diners, coffee shops, novelty shops and bars, and it proudly housed the largest grocery store in a thirty-mile radius. The little town of Neely, nestled in the center of the state of Iowa, was all Sarina knew.

Moisture began to bead on her forehead as Sarina peddled along the dry, dusty road. It was going to be a hot and humid Saturday, typical for that time of year. Wisps of long dark hair blew out behind Sarina despite her attempt to cinch it tightly into a ponytail.

Sarina rode with determination even though her shoulders were slumped forward with the weight of the weariness that seemed to surround her these days. She had often been told that her round face was pretty, especially when she smiled.

She was not smiling today.

Sarina was clad in one of her mother's outfits of a dark blue skirt that was a bit snug, a faded white blouse, and dark blue flats. But no stockings or socks as it was too hot for that. She carried a small bag on her back, which contained an apron, her purse, and a few extra items for tidying up once she got to her destination.

The bike started to crest a small hill in the road that overlooked the town in one direction, and another road leading out of this place in the other. Sarina always stopped at the top of the hill every time she rode into town and would either long for a way out or be thankful for the small town that she had grown up in. But not today. She was running late and couldn't afford to lose her job at the diner. She had not worked there long, only a few weeks in fact, but it was vital that she keep it. When her mother, Lucy Forester, had become too ill to work, Sarina had taken her place. She had been caring for her mother that morning and it had taken longer for Sarina to get away.

Sarina rode down the small hill, into town where the dusty road changed to pavement, and the perspiration from her neck soaked her collar. She hated to arrive at work drenched with sweat especially since she had to serve food to others, but Sarina refused to drive her car. Well, it was her mother's car, but Sarina drove it to the city once a month, so her mother could see specialists. The rest of the time Sarina rode her bike to help save on expenses. Lord knows she had plenty of those.

As Sarina drove down Main Street, Mavis Breecher called out a greeting of hello. Sarina smiled, lifted her hand, and waved.

"How's your mother?" Mavis asked.

Sarina stopped peddling and braked, setting her left foot on the ground. She never knew how to answer this question. Should she tell them the truth that her mother was dying, and it could be any day? Should she tell them she is doing as well as could be expected? Sarina realized she hadn't spoken yet and offered a sad smile. "She has good days and bad but is fighting."

"If you need anything let me know," Mavis said. Nodding her head as though saying goodbye, the older woman turned and walked down the sidewalk that nestled between the road and the connected row of shops.

"Thank you," Sarina called, watching the woman walk away. Sarina sighed and turned back to the task at hand and started pedaling toward the direction of the diner once more. Sarina rounded the next corner and passed the public accountant's office. She worked there during the week, and Sarina wished she were headed there instead of her current destination. She hated her second job at the diner, but it couldn't be helped. The doctor bills, medication expenses, and hospital bills were piling up. She was paying them off as quickly as possible, but it had become increasingly difficult when her mother couldn't work any longer. Sarina had to make the tough decision to take on her mother's old job at the diner, waiting tables, to help offset the growing expenses.

Sarina wondered if things might have been different if her father were still alive. Joe Forester had died in a car accident when Sarina was only six, and at times she found it difficult to remember him. Her mother used to tell her stories of how the farm had been prosperous, but that all changed when he died. They sold most of their land, leaving about twenty acres to lease for extra income and another five acres for them to have a small garden and keep their horses.

Times had been tough, but they managed. Sarina had even been set on going away to college, but when her mother found out she had cancer, all the money that had been saved for school had to go toward her mother's care. Her mother objected, of course, but Sarina couldn't fathom leaving or using that money for anything else. She loved her mother too much and told her she would attend community college and take classes online a little at a time, which is exactly what Sarina did.

Sarina worked and went to school and helped tend to her mother. Things seemed to be going well for a while and her mother even appeared to be getting better, but about a month ago, her mother took a turn for the worse and Sarina took over her mother's job and had to stop her classes. They also had to sell their horses and Sarina was contemplating selling the extra twenty acres.

A heavy sigh slipped out as Sarina arrived at the diner. She pulled around the side, toward the back, jumped off her bike and leaned it against the wall of the old building. Still rushing, she chained it to a pole that had once housed an American flag and walked in the side door of the diner. Everyone called a greeting to her and she called out her greetings in return. That was the thing about small towns, everyone knew everyone else and most were friendly to each other, to their faces anyway. Sarina walked toward the back of the dining room to a small hallway, where the bathroom was located. She freshened up and made her way back out and behind the diner's main counter to the kitchen and office, where she put her stuff in a small cubby. Pulling up her sleeves she jumped into her work.

It always amazed Sarina how fast time went by when the diner was busy. It had been several hours since she arrived and was almost time for her break when Sarina's neighbor boy, Todd Duncan, ran into the diner. He was tall and lanky and had an out-of-control mop of blond hair that stuck out on all sides of his baseball cap. He and his dad, Rick, had been working on repairing some boards on her front porch when Sarina left home, so she was startled when he rushed in. She started to call a greeting but the look on his face stopped her. Something was wrong. His normal bored-out-of-his-mind blue eyes had a look of fear and concern in them.

Sarina's heart began to pound, and she called to Trina to take over her table because she had to leave. She walked toward Todd and tried to ask a question but could not find the words. Todd nodded and motioned for Sarina to follow him. She tried to ask another question but instead turned and raced to the back, gathered her things, and returned to where Todd was waiting. Neither said a word as they left the diner. Todd put Sarina's bike into the back of his beat-up and once-blue truck and the two crawled into the cab, still without speaking.

They rode in silence the whole way to Sarina's house. Sarina tried and failed to stop her racing thoughts and calm her thundering heart. Todd pulled into the driveway, parked the truck, and jumped out of the cab. Sarina could not move—she was frozen.

The thought her mother might have died while she was gone terrified her.

Rick came out onto the porch as Todd rounded the truck to the passenger door. Rick walked slowly toward Sarina's side of the truck. He opened the door and reached out, grasping Sarina's hand softly. "Look at me, Sarina." Pausing long enough for Sarina to look his way, he continued, "She is still with us, but she doesn't have much longer."

Sarina looked at Rick, took a deep breath, wiped at her eyes, and nodded her understanding. As she started to get out of the truck Rick said, "The doctor is here and is getting her comfortable, but"—pausing again while a slight tear slid down his cheek—"she's been asking for you."

Sarina choked back the sobs that threatened to consume her and fought to stay calm. She was relieved her mother was still alive but dreaded the last conversation she would have with her. How could she cram all the *I love you*s, thoughts, and goodbyes into one last conversation? How was she supposed to deal with this? For several months Sarina had known this day was coming, and she had been trying to prepare herself, but now that this day had arrived, she felt completely lost and alone.

Her legs felt like lead as Sarina walked toward the porch, up the steps, and into the house. As her eyes adjusted to the dim room, Sarina noticed the doctor's wife, who she thought was named Lizzy, and Rick's wife, Mary, sitting on the couch in the living room.

They rose as Sarina walked toward them and they reached out as though to reassure her. She nodded her thanks, walked past them, her steps hesitant, into her mother's room. The doctor turned, the older man's eyes brimming with tears.

Another nice thing about a small town is that the doctor also knew everyone and there was a genuine care and concern for his patients. Her mother was no exception. But everyone loved her mother.

Her mother was not originally from Neely but had arrived as a young bride. She was from Italy, which was evident by her accent, but the community quickly embraced and accepted this kind, soft-spoken woman as one of their own. After all, she had married one of the town's pride and joys.

Sarina's father had been a football legend and had volunteered to serve his country. He had been in the middle of his service when he met her mother. When he returned home, he was a hero, and brought his new bride with him. He later became a successful farmer and prominent figure in the community. The day he died, the whole town mourned, and they would again with her mother's passing.

The doctor cleared his throat and Sarina crossed the room and grasped the outstretched hand. "How is she?" Sarina struggled to say.

He patted the top of Sarina's hand. "She's resting comfortably for now, but she fades in and out. She doesn't have much time left, my dear."

Nodding her head in understanding, Sarina said, "It's time for her to stop hurting."

"Yes," the doctor agreed. "She fought a long hard battle but it's time." Turning as though to leave the room, he added, "I will leave you now, she's been asking for you."

"Thank you."

Sarina waited for the doctor to close the door behind him before she moved to sit next to her mother. Cradling her mother's hand, she pulled it up to her lips for a gentle kiss. She reached over and brushed the dark and greying hair off her mother's forehead. "It's okay, Mama, I'm here now."

Her mother's eyes fluttered open, and she struggled to smile when she saw Sarina. "Oh, my sweet baby girl," she whispered and closed her eyes again. Sarina thought she had drifted back to sleep but her mother spoke again. "Sarina, please take my locket, my girl."

Sarina reached over and gently lifted the locket over her mother's head and placed it into her mother's palm. "Here you go, Mama."

Her mother smiled and said, "Oh honey, please open it for me, okay."

Obeying, Sarina grasped the locket and opened it to reveal a small picture of her mother's parents smiling at her. She had looked inside this locket so many times that their faces were as familiar as her own, but they were strangers to Sarina because her mother never spoke of them or her past.

"No, honey, there is a secret opening and I want you to open that for me."

Sarina studied the locket. *How many times have I looked at these faces, held this locket, and never realized there was a secret opening?* Sarina found what she thought might release it and pressed. Sure enough, the locket sprung open a second time and a small key fell into Sarina's lap.

Gasping, Sarina picked it up and studied it. It was an old key, and one she had never seen before.

"What is this, Mama," Sarina whispered.

Her mother looked over at Sarina and tried to open her eyes, but they were too heavy, and she closed them again, which appeared to frustrate her mother.

Wanting to calm her, Sarina said, "It's okay, Mama, we can do this later."

"We don't have a later, my darling girl," her mother whispered with a fierceness that belied her condition.

It was all Sarina could do to keep from crying out. Instead, a tear rolled down her cheek. "Okay, Mama. What is this key to?"

Her mother lay still, her eyes were closed, and Sarina worried this was the end. But her mother opened her eyes and took a deep breath. "Look in my hope chest and wrapped in my old quilt is a box. Please, go, do it now."

Puzzled, Sarina stood and walked over to the chest at the foot of her bed. She opened the lid and caught the strong scent of cedar that lined the inside. Memories flooded Sarina, of helping her mother look for pictures, her mother's favorite trinkets, and the old quilt.

Sarina dug to the bottom where she felt the quilt and pulled it out. She was surprised by the weight of it and glanced at her mother. Sarina unwrapped the quilt, revealing a box. It was larger than Sarina expected, and she stared at it, wondering at its contents.

Pulling herself to the task at hand, Sarina carried the box to the chair beside her mother and sat while she continued to study the box, fingering the small lock. She lifted the key and looked over at her mother who now had her eyes open, studying her intently.

Mother and daughter stared at each other until her mother said, "Go ahead, sweetheart. Open it."

Sarina's hand trembled as she inserted the key and turned her hand. The click of the lock releasing startled her, but she recovered quickly and opened the lid. "What is this, Mama?"

"It's my past, Sarina, and it is what I believe to be your future."

"What do you mean?"

"You will see pictures in there—some you have seen, some you have not. You will also find my favorite pictures of your father. But mostly you will find pictures and keepsakes of the place that was once my home."

Sarina lifted one picture that caught her attention. It was a picture of her mother and father. They both looked so young and incredibly happy and they appeared to be standing on a ridge that overlooked a small town nestled between the side of a hill and water. The blue of the water was breathtaking and so was the happiness that showed on her parents' faces.

"Where is this place?"

"It's the small village in Italy where I grew up. Vetualini."

"Why have you never shown me this?"

"Oh, honey, the circumstances under which I left that place were so difficult and your father gave me such hope for a new start and a better place. For years it hurt to talk about, and when the pain subsided, I could never find the words. My one regret was not taking you sooner to see it, but perhaps it is better this way."

"How could it be better this way?"

The failing woman reached across and grasped Sarina's hand weakly. "My own fears were too powerful to return, but I believe with all my heart that you must go. Do the thing I was never strong enough to do and go."

"How could going now even be a consideration? I am so confused. I don't even know what questions to ask."

"You will learn my darkest secret soon enough. For now, though, you must promise me that you will go."

"Neely is my home, not some place in a picture. Mama, I don't know if—"

"You must go, Sarina!" her mother snapped. "You must promise me this!" She struggled to sit up, reaching for her daughter.

Not wanting to upset her mother further and not even knowing how she would keep this promise, Sarina reassured her that she would go. This seemed to calm her mother as she lay back down and stared at the ceiling. Sarina jumped when her mother started to talk about her village as though she had just been there yesterday. She spoke of its people, its culture, its traditions, and Sarina could almost picture her mother standing in the middle of her village while she explained everything in such vivid detail.

They continued to talk about her mother's childhood home, and Sarina asked questions when it was appropriate to do so. They laughed when a funny story was told and cried when her mother was saddened by a distant memory that brought back the knowledge that she would never see it again. Her mother shared more about her life in Italy in those few moments than her mother had ever shared before. Sarina was puzzled by this at first but thought perhaps when one reaches the end of their life, they reflect on its beginning. Soon her mother grew weary and started to fall back to sleep. Sarina thought she had drifted off again, but her mother opened her eyes and their eyes locked.

"Just a few more words, my dear sweet daughter." She paused as though to catch her breath before she continued. "I love you more than life itself. You are a strong, brave woman, and you will live a long happy life, I know this. You must do as you promised and go to Vetualini. I just know you will find your future there. I know you have always felt lost here. I belonged here with your father, but you, my precious daughter, belong there. And please find a resting place for my ashes in Vetualini."

"Your ashes?"

"Yes, my darling. You must take my ashes to Vetualini and find a resting place for me there. Promise me this."

"I promise, Mama," Sarina agreed.

"Thank you for giving me such joy and happiness in my life, my sweet girl, as I know I did not deserve it. I love you, and I will always be with you."

Sarina did not know when she had started to cry but knew she must have been doing it for a while. Her cheeks were streaked, and the tears that had dropped from her chin had dampened her shirt. Sarina held her mother's hand and continued to cry in the silence that was now present.

Her mother did not speak again, and not long after, she died. The pain she had once, was no more. Although Sarina was relieved her mother would no longer suffer, she mourned for the woman who was her whole life. She felt completely lost and alone.

Chapter Two

There was a faint knock on the front door and Sarina almost didn't hear it until it came a second time. It had been two days since her mother died. Sarina stood in her kitchen surrounded by food and flowers, and she wasn't sure what she was going to do with it all. Mourners continued to stop by unannounced, so this time she didn't want to answer the door. Many in her small community were saddened by her mother's death, but Sarina wanted to be left alone.

Her mother's voice in her head told her to be polite, so she walked from the kitchen to the front door. Sarina grabbed the knob, took a deep breath, and opened it. She forced a smile and prepared for an onslaught of *I'm sorrys* and tears and more ham and potato casserole or another cake. But what she got was Bob Tanner smiling.

He didn't have food in hand, and he didn't immediately say, "I'm sorry." Instead, he said, "I know this is a tough time, but I just had to come by to make sure you are okay."

Sarina opened the screen door and hugged the man who had been her father's best friend. When they pulled apart, Bob looked down at her. "How are you holding up?"

"Okay, I guess," Sarina said as she backed up enough for the older man to walk past her into the house. Sarina shut the front door and led the way to the kitchen. She found herself asking, "Are you hungry or thirsty? I have plenty of food."

"That is one thing this town is especially good at," Bob said. "They know how to cook and give when a family is in need."

Sarina nodded, went to the cupboard, and pulled out two plates and two glasses and set them on the table. As she lifted the pitcher to pour the lemonade, Bob waved his hand in the air and said, "I'm not hungry, and I don't need anything to drink."

"Are you sure. I really don't see how I am going to eat all this"—gesturing to all the food scattered around the kitchen—"by myself."

"I'm sure, but please go ahead."

Sarina nodded, put the second glass and both plates away, and poured herself a glass of lemonade. She took a sip and sat at the kitchen table.

Bob sat across from Sarina and asked, "Do you need anything? Do you need help with the, um"— clearing his throat—"the arrangements?"

"No, I'm okay. Mom and I prepared a lot of things ahead of time, so it was just a matter of making some phone calls and finalizing a few details."

"Well, let me know if that changes and if you need anything. I am only a phone call away."

"Of course, thank you."

"Any thoughts of what you're going to do next?" Bob asked, changing the subject. "I know you were planning on going to college and that got put on hold. Do you think you might pursue that now?"

"I honestly don't know," Sarina said. "I haven't even thought about it. I'm just wanting to get through the next couple of days, then I'll start making some decisions."

"Well, that's a good idea. You never want to make rash or hasty decisions ..." Bob trailed off, his face turning red. Taking a deep breath he said, "I didn't mean to imply that you are being rash or hasty or anything, or that you already have your next steps in life mapped out. I just want to help any way that I can, and—this isn't coming out right."

Bob and Sarina's father had grown up together in Neely. They had been football legends together. Gone to college together. Served their country together. And at one point, Sarina's father had saved Bob's life. Because of the history the two men shared, Sarina knew her family held a special place in Bob's heart.

Sarina was touched by his show of concern even if he was clumsy in delivering it. She giggled and said, "It didn't seem to come out wrong to me." Seeing the look of relief wash across the older man's face Sarina asked, "How is your family doing?"

"They're doing okay. But we're all saddened by your mother's passing."

"I appreciate that so much. She was so loved."

"Yes, she was. A great member of this community. She will be missed as your father is."

"Hmm, my father. I am glad they are together again. No doubt dancing with joy that they are reunited." Sarina bowed her head and fiddled with her cup. Everything around her grew hazy as the moisture in her eyes tried to seep out. She swallowed the lump in her throat and took another sip of lemonade.

Bob reached across the table and squeezed Sarina's hand. "I must get going, Sarina, but please—please don't hesitate to reach out for anything. I mean it. We're here if you need anything. Anything at all."

Sarina looked over at Bob and her lips curved upward. She could feel the dampness swell in her eyes again, so she swallowed and wiped her face with her hand. "I so appreciate your kindness. Thank you so much for stopping by. I have a meeting with the minister to finalize a few things regarding Mama's service so I will walk you out."

They both stood and Sarina walked over to the sink. She started rinsing out her glass when Bob cleared his throat and said, "You, of course, have so much to do. And I don't want to be in your way. I just wanted to stop by real quick and let you know we are here for ya."

Sarina dried her hands, walked across the room, and placed her hand on Bob's arm. "I know my mother would be thankful that you did."

A small tear slid down the man's face, so out of character for the gruff old rancher that Sarina had to fight hard not to tear up again. She knew she had to stay strong but was not expecting this man's tender response to her mother's passing.

The two walked to the doorway of the kitchen arm in arm. Bob stopped, leaned down and kissed Sarina on the cheek. "No need to walk me out. Just remember we are only a phone call away."

Sarina nodded and watched Bob walk toward the front door. He hollered one final goodbye and was gone. Sarina crossed the living room and looked out the window just as Bob was pulling out of her driveway in his truck. She stood staring after him until he disappeared down the road. Even though the truck was gone, she continued to stare out at the road for far too long. Shivering, Sarina pulled herself out of her trance and rushed to find her purse and items needed for the meeting with the minister. She was going to be late.

Why does it always seem to rain on the day of funerals? Sarina wondered as she looked outside her kitchen window. She finished drinking the last of her coffee and set her mug in the sink with a clank. She almost left it as is but hearing her mother's voice in her head telling her to wash it and put it away, Sarina did just that. She would have a house full of people after the funeral, so it was better this way anyway.

After washing the mug and putting it away, Sarina scanned the small kitchen to make sure everything was neat and tidy. The butcher block counters were scuffed from years of use, but they were clean with only a small cookie jar, coffee pot, and catch-all basket sitting neatly on them. The farmhouse sink gleamed from the quick wipe down. Thankfully, her small kitchen table was now empty of all the food and flowers from before and it now held the usual round doily as a center piece. The stove, which was at the end of the counter to the right of the sink, was clean, but old and battered. Not much she could do about that.

The fridge made a small noise and Sarina looked over at it, making sure the outer surface was clean. It stood proudly to the left of the back door as though it knew it was the newest appliance in the room. Sarina walked over and checked for dust or streaks on the large window that was on the top half of the back door. She fingered the white lace curtains her mother had made years ago and smiled at the memory of her mother making them to match the curtains over the sink.

Sarina glanced over at the door that led to her mother's room and thought maybe she should make sure it was clean. Not really wanting to go in there, she changed her mind. She looked down at the simple tiled floors to make sure she had remembered to sweep them and wondered if she should have washed the rugs that were scattered around. It was too late to do that now, so she shrugged and said, "They will have to do." Sarina felt proud at the tidiness of the kitchen.

Sarina walked into the living room and looked at the clock. She realized she would arrive early at the church, so she sat on her couch. The room was only slightly bigger than the kitchen. With the bookcase, a few chairs, the china cabinet, the two end tables and the couch, she wondered how she was going to fit everyone in there. The wall to the right of the couch had a large fireplace with a dark wood mantel lined with various photos of captured memories. Sarina stood and walked across the room to stare at the photos but caught her reflection in the small TV hanging above the mantel.

Dark and empty eyes stared back at her. She flinched and wondered if there would ever be life in them again.

Sarina turned to avoid her reflection and did one final mental check that the room was tidy. She forced a smile and tried to not think about her feelings, but she saw her mother and the life her mother had built in every part of the room. She could almost see her mom sitting in her favorite chair close to the fire. It was eerie how much she could feel her mother's presence even though she was gone. The farm had not been her mother's heritage, but her mother had made it her own.

The small farmhouse had been built by Sarina's great, great grandparents and they passed it on to the next generation. It continued to be passed down until it became her father's, then her mother's when he died. Now it was Sarina's.

Sarina frowned, remembering that it had always made her mother a little sad that she could not maintain the vibrant farm it had once been. Over the years there had been offers for assistance to make it a booming farm again, but her mother always turned them down. She believed it would have been charity to accept and her mother said she couldn't stand for that. There was one time Bob had offered to help and Sarina remembered her mother saying, "We will make our own way, Sarina, and we will make your father proud with what we do, no matter what it is."

When her mother got sick, Sarina received the same offers to help, but Sarina's response was much the same as her mother's and she turned them down. Bob had the biggest voice in offering to help. And Sarina had told him the same thing her mother had told her. "We will make our own way."

Sarina chuckled, remembering Bob stopping by just to remind her that he and his family were there for her. She was sure he would offer to help with the farm as time passed. She knew that because of their history, Bob thought it was his duty to help. But Sarina and her mother never accepted help before, and Sarina wouldn't start, even now.

Sarina looked back at the mantel, at the picture of her father standing proud in his uniform, her mother next to him, smiling up at him. Sarina wished they were both here, but her wishing wouldn't make it so. Her shoulders slumped forward with the weight of the emptiness in the room, so she decided to leave. She didn't care if she got to the church early. She just didn't want to be alone with her memories another moment.

Ten minutes later, Sarina pulled into the church parking lot. She crinkled her eyebrows and frowned at the sight of several cars. At the prospect of seeing other people, she forgot her loneliness and her reasons for going to the church. She realized she had not fled to escape loneliness or the memories. Sarina needed a few moments alone with her mother, one last time.

Sarina found a spot close to the church's front entrance, pulled into it and parked her car. The rain drops fell softly as she climbed out of the driver's seat. She paused, looked around at the rolling Iowa farmland that surrounded the church, and smiled. This view had always been a favorite of her mother's. But not wanting to get too damp, Sarina turned, walked to the front entrance, and made her way inside.

There was no one in the sanctuary when Sarina walked in and she sighed. She walked to the casket that cradled her mother and peered in. They would be cremating her after the service, but Sarina thought it best that people got to say their goodbyes to her and not her ashes. It was the only thing Sarina had done different from her mother's wishes. But she knew her mother would understand that this was for Sarina and the town and not for her mother.

Her mother's face looked like a doll with the makeup they had used to hide the blemishes that came with death. Sarina let the tears flow unchecked down her cheeks. She felt so lost and alone, and she had no idea how she would carry on.

"What am I going to do, Mama?" Sarina whispered.

A dash of remembrance sprang to mind. The promise she made to her mother.

Italy.

A door slamming in the distance startled Sarina and she turned as someone walked into the sanctuary behind her. "Oh, Sarina. I didn't realize you were already here."

Sarina squinted her eyes at the woman approaching and realized that it was the reverend's wife. *Of course, she would be here*, Sarina thought to herself.

Sarina smiled at the short plump woman and said, "Hello Mrs. Davies. I hope I didn't surprise you. I just wanted to see Mama one more time before ..." Sarina trailed off.

"Of course, my dear. Of course," Mrs. Davies replied. "You take all the time you want. I will be in the pastor's study if you need me."

"Okay. Thank you."

Sarina watched the kind woman walk out of sight and turned back to her mother. She stared at her mother's face and whispered about memories, said her goodbyes and finally said, "I love you always." Sarina grew weak, but when she turned and tried to walk, her legs felt like she was moving through a thick bog. She had to force each step forward until she reached the nearest pew and collapsed into it.

She didn't know how long she sat in the silence, letting the tears flow, but eventually her cheeks felt tight from where the dampness had long since dried and she could hear people entering the sanctuary behind her. Sarina glanced at the growing crowd as Mrs. Davies sat next to her.

"It's time," she whispered.

Mrs. Davies helped Sarina to her feet and over to the casket. She squeezed Sarina's hand and walked away, leaving Sarina to stand alone and wait for the onslaught.

It didn't take long for Sarina to be surrounded by those who had come to pay their respects before the service started. Some wept, some reminisced, and some hugged Sarina not saying anything. And everyone said their goodbyes to her mother. Sarina smiled when she was supposed to smile, cried when it became hard not to hold back the tears, but even though she was surrounded by so many people, she felt so out of place and alone.

After the parade of mourners had passed through to say their goodbyes, they all sat in their respective seats and waited. Sarina looked down at her mother, took a deep breath and returned to her seat. She only had to wait a few minutes for the pastor to begin the funeral service.

The service was a short one, per the wishes of her mother, but Sarina thought it would never end. The longer she sat there the more lost she felt. The whole experience seemed surreal, and she grappled with it. When Sarina thought she couldn't bear another moment, the pastor was closing with a final prayer.

After the prayer was over, Sarina was to go and say goodbye to her mother for the last time. Instead, she stood as though frozen in place.

Mrs. Davies put her arm around Sarina and said, "Go on, my dear."

Sarina nodded her head and tried to move. But every step forward was a thousand pounds on her legs, and she thought she would never make it across the short distance. She finally stood over her mother, and she caressed her mother's cheek while her knees threatened to buckle beneath her. Sarina's head bowed and her shoulders slumped forward as her heart broke into a thousand pieces. Tears ran down her face unchecked and she choked on the sobs that rushed out of her.

Sarina grabbed the casket as her body swayed and she felt arms wrap around her body. She considered collapsing into the warmth of the embrace but felt strength rise inside her and resisted the urge. She forced herself to calm, let go of the casket, and said a final goodbye to her mother.

Sarina glanced at Mrs. Davies, who still had one arm wrapped around her shoulders, and said, "I'm ready."

Mrs. Davies nodded, let go of Sarina, and escorted her to the foyer.

"Do you need a minute?" Mrs. Davies asked, while the two took their places in a corner of the room.

Taking a deep breath, Sarina said, "No, I am feeling better now. More composed."

"Okay, but I will stand next to you this time, so you are not alone."

"Thank you."

The two women faced the townspeople for the next hour before gathering their things to head to Sarina's home. Mrs. Davies offered to drive Sarina home, but she declined and said, "See you there.

Normally the townspeople would come by after the burial, but since Sarina's mother was being cremated, everyone was heading over to Sarina's house straight from the church to drop off food and visit with her for several more hours. Sarina was sure some of the ladies, those closest to her mother, were already at the little farmhouse preparing it for guests.

Several minutes later, Sarina pulled into her driveway and confirmed her earlier belief that her mother's friends were already at her house preparing for the invasion. *That description seems a bit harsh*, Sarina thought to herself. But it felt like an invasion because after the emotions of the past couple of hours, all she wanted was to be left alone.

Sarina parked on the side of the driveway to leave room for other people to park. She climbed out of the driver's seat and rushed into her house to avoid getting wet from the rain that continued to fall. Sarina called a greeting as she entered her living room.

"We are back here, Sarina," Mavis Breecher yelled.

Sarina squeezed into her kitchen which hummed with Lizzy, Mary, and Darla Tanner all scuttling about the kitchen preparing for the town to stop by. She caught the faint scent of pie crust burning and half expected her mother to burst into the room shouting she was burning it again. Sarina giggled as memories flooded her thoughts and watched Mary pull out the source of the aroma. She breathed in the smell of cinnamon and apples as the oven door slammed shut.

It was her mother's favorite.

"What can I do to help," Sarina asked.

"Nothing, you go sit, and breathe, before everyone gets here," Darla said, hugging Sarina quickly as she passed by with a platter of meat and cheese.

Sarina watched for another moment, shrugged her shoulders, and went to the living room. She sat on her couch and leaned back, sinking as far as she could into the cushions. She closed her eyes briefly but sighed when she heard the crunch of tires driving over gravel. Her eyes flew open, she stood and said, "Here we go."

Sarina welcomed the comfort at first, but soon grew tired of it all and managed not to let her impatience show. Most seemed to struggle to say something, and she thought maybe they didn't know what to say, because she heard all the same sentiments. Sarina accepted every hug, every "I'm sorry" and every "find peace in your memories." She soon found it ironic how earlier in the day she felt lonely and didn't want to be alone, but now, that was all she wanted.

Maybe it's because even though I am surrounded by people I still feel lonely. And I would rather be by myself and lonely, then in a crowd of people and lonely. She forced all her thoughts of loneliness aside and focused on the next hug and the next sentiment until the minutes turned into hours, and everyone started to say their goodbyes one by one.

Sarina stood on her front porch waving at the last car pulling out of her driveway. When the car turned on to the dirt road that led into town, she walked back into her house, shutting the door behind her. She looked around the room and it was just as it had been that morning when she left for church. Even though she'd had a house full of people for the last few hours, it didn't look like it.

"Well, that's one thing to be thankful for," Sarina mumbled as her eyes grew heavy. She decided she had enough of the day.

She took off her shoes and stumbled her way up the stairs to her bedroom. Sarina pulled off her dress on her way to the bed and crawled in. She sank into the sheets and pulled them over her. The sorrow and emotions of the day weighed on her as her head rested on the pillow and it didn't take long for her to fall asleep.

Chapter Three

Sarina lifted her head off her pillow and looked around. She wasn't sure how long she had slept. Peeking out her bedroom window, she saw it was barely light outside. Thinking she had slept only a few hours, Sarina grabbed her alarm clock. It wasn't dusk, it was dawn. She had slept the rest of the day and all through the night. It was the most sleep she'd had in weeks, but instead of feeling refreshed, Sarina felt groggy. She put the clock back in its designated spot on the nightstand, closed her eyes and went back to sleep.

Several hours later, the sound of a distant tractor pulled Sarina out of her slumber. She looked at her alarm clock and realized it was almost noon. She pushed back the covers and forced herself to get out of bed. She went through the routine of using the bathroom and taking a shower, but she felt numb, lost and she hated how the loneliness overwhelmed her. Sarina burst into tears, her shoulders shaking with every sob. Her sorrow poured out of her heart with every tear that fell, and the warm water from her shower washed it all away.

After Sarina had cried until she couldn't cry any more, she finished her shower feeling more refreshed and lighter. Perhaps it was the shower or the extra sleep that made her feel this way, but Sarina couldn't help but think it was the pain of losing her mother being washed away with her tears.

Sarina dressed in her favorite leggings, an oversized t-shirt, decided against a bra, and went to the kitchen to make lunch. The sun radiated into the room from the window over the sink, and the bright blue sky beckoned her outside. She gathered her lunch, went out to the back porch, and sat at the little table nestled in the corner. Sarina ate her ham and cheese sandwich while gazing out toward the fields.

Oh, how I wish I hadn't sold our horses. This would have been a perfect time to ride. She knew, of course, that all she had to do was ask any of her neighbors to let her ride one of their horses, but Sarina didn't feel like talking to anyone just yet. Plus, it wouldn't be the same, so she let that thought go.

She finished her lunch, pushed her plate away and sipped the rest of her lemonade. As time ticked by slowly, Sarina became restless. She went back inside to her mother's room. Sarina emerged a few minutes later and carried her mother's keepsake box to the small table.

Sarina removed the key from the locket resting around her neck and unlocked the box. Her hands shook as she lifted the lid. Seeing the picture on top, she snapped it shut. Sarina took big gulping breaths, trying not to panic.

A single tear slid down her right cheek and she wiped it away as she gained control of her breathing. She steadied her hands and slowly lifted the lid. Her heart pounded again as she pulled out the picture— the one of her mother and father she'd looked at on the day of her mother's death. They seemed so alive and happy in this picture, and it made Sarina's heart ache.

Sarina's mother was much younger in this picture—same dark curly hair, same brown eyes, and same beautiful smile—as the woman she knew. She had always been a slender woman and several inches shorter than Sarina. Her handsome father was all but laughing as he held his young wife. He wore his uniform and his brown hair and blue eyes shown from the sunny day. Or was it happiness that brightened his appearance?

Sarina sighed and felt a rush of warmth at their joy. She grew curious about what else was in the box, so she set the picture aside and sifted through pictures of strange places and unfamiliar people and studied each of them. Sarina reached into the box once more and discovered an envelope. It had her name on it.

Sarina paused, and with trembling hands lifted the envelope out of the box as though it would break if she dropped it. She laid the envelope on the table and stared at it.

Sarina was desperate for some sort of contact from her mother and here it was, but she was afraid to open it, afraid to read it and be done with it, because it would be their last contact. The finality scared her. After a few minutes of fighting the conflict raging inside her, she snatched up the envelope and tore it open. She pulled out the letter, held it close to her heart, took a deep breath and was overcome by the smell of her mother's favorite body lotion.

"Oh!" Sarina exclaimed while memories poured through her. With shaking hands, she unfolded the letter, breathed in her mother's scent once more, and began to read.

> My Darling Daughter,
> It pains me to write this letter to you today as I know that when you will finally read it, I will be gone and you will be alone and in pain, and for that reason my heart aches for you. I was given a gift so long ago when your

father came into my life and loved me as he did. And then you were born, and I honestly believed I couldn't love anyone more deeply than I loved you and your father.

Loss is a hard thing in life to deal with, especially when it is the loss of someone you love most of all. I know this as I experienced it as you are experiencing it now. I could try to provide words of comfort but that is all they would be right now, just words. But in time, you will find peace again and I know you will find love.

I know even as you read this letter you are struggling with what direction to take in your life. Please remember the promise you will make to me. I fully believe that promise will lead you to where you are meant to go. It will take you on the journey that is meant for you. Your destiny. Your fate. You have so much to offer in this life, my sweet girl, and you can no longer stay in our tiny little house in our tiny little town.

This is your time. Take it! Take it without fear even when at times it is scary. You will learn things about me on

this journey, and I pray that you find
the truth in it and I hope you can still
love me and remember me for who I was
in my life with you and your father and
not who I was then.

Now you may be wondering how to
start this new journey of yours. It will
begin with a single phone call. It will be
a phone call to your grandmother, someone who you have never met or spoken
with, but she will be someone who will
welcome you with open arms. You must
call her and let her know I am gone. And
you must tell her you are coming. This
will be the start of your journey.

Remember, you are a brave and
strong woman. And you are not alone. I
will always be with you. Please keep your
promise to me as I know it is what is
meant for you.

I love you, my sweet, sweet girl!
Your Mama

Laying the letter in front of her, she contemplated
what she read. Her mother had known Sarina would
promise to go to Italy before they had even discussed
it. Other thoughts and phrases ran through her mind,
while she tried to make sense of it all—call your

grandmother, keep your promise, you will learn things, and I hope you can still love me. What did it all mean and how could her mother ever believe for a moment that she could stop loving her?

Even though she was confused, Sarina knew she had to fulfill her promise to her mother, but right now she couldn't face it. Right now, she wanted to go back inside and crawl under her covers and hide from it all. So that is exactly what she did.

Sarina stared at the phone in her hand. She had typed in the number to her grandmother's home in Vetualini but couldn't bring herself to tap on the final button that would start the call. She took a deep breath, lightly touched the last button, and held the phone to her ear. She heard it ringing but no one answered right away. Sarina was about to disconnect the call when she heard a voice, so she put the phone back to her ear. Sarina wasn't sure what the woman was saying because she was speaking Italian.

Sarina hoped that whoever was on the other line could speak English. "Hello. Is this the Giacoletti household?"

There was a pause on the other end. "Yes, this is," the woman answered with an accent.

"Um, my name is Sarina, um Sarina Forester. Do you know who I am?"

The woman on the line started to shout in Italian to someone in the background. Sarina could hear movement. "You are my granddaughter."

Sarina felt relieved and started to ask another question, but her grandmother asked, "Is she gone? Is my daughter gone?"

Sarina's eyes filled with tears and asked, "How did you—"

"She is my daughter, child. And she told me that her time was coming soon."

"I never knew—"

"That she talked with me? She was always running from her haunted past. And you were her new future. She didn't like the two lives to mingle. But she couldn't let go of her mammina."

Sarina knew she would have felt the same way and smiled at the thought. She took a deep breath to gain courage. "Would it be okay if I came to see you?"

Sarina heard the other woman start crying as she choked out, "God be praised she is coming home to us. Cosimo, she is coming home. Quando?" Her grandmother slipped into Italian again but switched to English as though she realized Sarina wouldn't understand. "When?"

"I am finishing the details but hope to be there by next month."

"Sarina, you must keep in touch with me. Let me know as soon as you have made your travel arrangements. We will be preparing for your arrival."

They talked about a few more things and said their goodbyes. Sarina took the phone away from her ear to disconnect the call, but she could still hear her grandmother say, "Oh God be praised she is finally coming home to us."

A wave of excitement washed over her, and Sarina felt a little less lonely. She felt like she had a purpose or a direction. Perhaps her mother was right. Perhaps she was finally moving toward her destiny. Sarina frowned as she thought about the part in her mother's letter that concerned her—the secret—the one that might change things between them. She shuddered and couldn't stand the thought. Sarina shifted her thoughts to her grandmother's excitement, pushed the unease as far down as she could, and focused on what needed to happen next.

She was going to Italy!

Chapter Four

Sarina stood back and looked around the room after zipping her last suitcase. She had no idea what to bring so she packed a little of everything: pants, jeans, shorts, dresses, skirts, shirts, blouses, several types of shoes, and the list went on. She almost forgot her swimsuit, but remembered it in the last minute. She also threw in her mother's favorite wrap and dark blue sweater—the few of her items that fit Sarina and still smelled faintly of lavender and thyme soap.

Sarina decided to take a couple of photo albums filled with memories of the life her family had here in Iowa, in case her grandmother wanted to see them. She put those in a separate suitcase along with her favorite photo of her mother, the last picture of her father and her mother's urn. And of course, she packed the keepsake box. She was concerned it wouldn't fit, but after some rearranging, she was able to put it in her largest suitcase, wrapped in a thin blanket with some of her clothes tucked in around it.

A sense of unease mixed with excitement filled her, but Sarina took a deep breath, picked up her carry-on bags and went downstairs. It took three trips to get all her luggage downstairs, and she was sweating when the chore was completed. She left everything in the living room and went into the kitchen for a glass of water.

Sarina put her glass in the sink and glanced around the room to confirm it was tidy. She grabbed an apple from the fruit bowl on the counter and munched on it as she walked around the house, mentally checking off an imaginary list as she went. She double checked that her passport and plane tickets were neatly tucked in their designated spots, and heard two vehicles pull into her driveway.

Sarina threw away what was left of her apple, washed her hands, and opened the front door. Todd was taking her to the airport, and it appeared that Rick and Mary wanted to come and say goodbye. Sarina waved and called, "Hello," when they stepped out of their cars.

Mary walked on to the porch and gave Sarina a long hug. "Your mother would be so proud that you are doing this, Sarina. She so wanted this for you."

Sarina pulled back and frowned. "You knew about this?"

"Why of course, we talked about a lot of things. Most of all we talked about what was to come of you after she was gone. She loved you so much. I'm glad you are going. We'll miss you, but this is a good thing."

"Thank you," Sarina said and turned to Todd. "There are three rather large suitcases at the bottom of the stairs and two carry-on bags."

Mary motioned to her son to hurry up and turned back to Sarina. "Do you need anything, or can we do anything while you are gone?"

"Well," Sarina said hesitantly, "would you mind terribly, checking on the house to make sure nothing goes wrong while I am gone? I asked the post office to hold my mail and any packages for me, but you might keep an eye on that just in case as well. If that's okay?"

"Of course, happy to help."

"Oh, there is some food and milk left in the fridge and freezer. Please feel free to take what you want. It isn't a lot, but I hate to throw it out if you can use it. Just throw away anything you don't want."

"Thank you, we will do that."

Mary walked past Sarina into the house and on to the kitchen. Sarina followed, rummaged in a cabinet, found a paper sack, and handed it to Mary. She watched as Mary filled it with the few items left in the fridge and freezer—some meat and vegetables, a half-gallon of milk, some cheese, a few eggs, and a few apples. After Mary was done, the two women walked back into the living room. Mary continued to the front door, but Sarina stopped. Her suitcases were loaded, and she stared at the empty space where they had been sitting.

"You okay, honey?" Mary asked.

"Huh, oh yes," Sarina said. "I just realized, I'm scared to death and excited and frightened and worried and happy and—and ..." She trailed off and shrugged.

"Of course, you are"—Mary closed the distance between them, adjusted the groceries and put her free arm around Sarina—"but it will be fine. You, will be fine." Mary pulled away and shifted the groceries once more. "I'm going to take these out to our car. Come on out when you're ready, okay."

Sarina nodded and watched Mary walk out the front door. She turned about the room, took a deep breath, gathered her purse, and turned one more time. "Goodbye house." She walked out the front door and locked it behind her.

The trip to the airport was only an hour, but to Sarina, it felt much longer. The closer they got, the stronger the butterflies fluttered in her stomach. She had never flown before, let alone to another country, and here she was doing it by herself.

She had an idea of what to expect since Mary, and even Todd, had explained how things worked, but she still felt nervous and hoped she wouldn't do anything embarrassing. When they arrived at the airport, Todd pulled along the curb in front of the doors to Sarina's airline. He jumped out of the truck and she saw him go and run to snag a luggage cart.

Sarina took a deep breath and placed a hand on her fluttering stomach, attempting to calm it. She watched in the rear-view mirror as Todd pulled out and stacked each suitcase and carry-on bag neatly on the cart.

He pushed the cart forward, glanced at his truck, and opened Sarina's door. "You going to get out?"

Sarina felt frozen in place.

Todd leaned toward her and asked, "You sure you don't want me to walk you in at least? Show you where to go?"

Sarina forced a grin. "No, I think I will be fine. Thank you for bringing me, helping me with the bags." She climbed out of the truck. "Oh, can I give you some cash?"

Todd scrunched his nose. "Nah, my mom would kill me."

Sarina laughed and hugged him. They had never been close or even friends really, but Sarina wanted to hug the last contact she had with her home and the known.

"Uh, you okay, Sarina?"

"Yes, I think I am. Goodbye Todd, and thanks again."

"Sure." Todd jogged to his truck, jumped in, and meandered into traffic.

Sarina watched him drive away out of sight before turning toward her bags and the great unknown.

Two hours later, she walked onto the plane. She had decided to fly first class. It was a splurge, but she felt like she deserved the little extra considering everything. She would probably fly home via coach, but today she was going to go in style.

It didn't take long for Sarina to find her seat. She stowed her carry-on bags, gathered her book to keep her preoccupied on the flight, and sat down. She felt jittery as she glanced outside and was glad she chose a window seat. Her hands shook as she fumbled with the seat belt and she could feel sweat building on her forehead. Relief washed over her when she finally heard it click into place.

She looked out her tiny window again and watched the ground crew bustle around doing their various tasks to prepare the plane for take-off. While suit-cases were being loaded, she tried to find hers but heard someone talking behind her. She turned to-ward the voice and realized it was one of the flight attendants asking if she needed anything to drink be-fore takeoff.

Sarina smiled. "Um, no thank you, I am fine for now."

"Well, you just push the flight attendant button if you need anything."

Sarina nodded and thanked her.

She watched the flight attendant walk to the next person, turned and looked back out her little window. This was all so new to Sarina, and she was excited. She was flying to New York City first, would transfer planes there, then fly to Florence, Italy. That would put Sarina in Italy the following morning.

Her mother's family lived in the Tuscany region along the coast of the Tyrrhenian Sea, and it was cheaper to fly into Florence and drive to their village of Vetualini. Sarina had no idea who would be meet-ing her at the airport, but her grandmother reassured her that someone would be there to greet her. Excite-ment bubbled at the prospect of her journey until she felt the jolt of the plane backing away from the gate and felt butterflies again. *What am I doing? Flying to the other side of the world by myself to see strangers? What if they don't like me? What if they hated Mama because of that terrible secret, and what if—What if—What if …*

Sarina took a deep breath, placed her hand on her heart and tried not to panic, while she watched the ground grow smaller and smaller.

It wasn't long before the captain announced, "Feel free to move about the cabin."

Sarina was still trying to breathe normally when the same flight attendant stopped in front of her and asked, "Are you okay, miss?"

She took another deep breath and felt her face soften. "Um yes, it's my first time flying."

"Ah, I see. Would you like for me to get you a cocktail? It might help calm your nerves."

Sarina agreed, thanked the flight attendant, and looked back out the window.

When the flight attendant returned, she held a small glass filled with a pale pink liquid. It had a tiny straw sticking out of it that twirled around when she handed the beverage to Sarina. "Here you go, miss. Enjoy."

Sarina took the drink offered, thanked the flight attendant a second time, had a small thought—*is it too early for this?*—and drank the cocktail. She let the warmth of it wash over her, relaxed in her seat, and closed her eyes. *Nope, not too early at all.*

The rest of the flight was uneventful, and Sarina was surprised when the captain announced they were descending into the Big Apple. Sarina looked out at the magnificent skyscrapers. They appeared to be rising to meet her. The sun reflected off various walls of glass, adding a sparkle to the backdrop of concrete. She wished she had time to explore this amazing looking city, but her next flight was to take off in a few hours.

Several hours later, Sarina was on her next flight, settled in her seat and reading her book. When the flight attendant paused in front of her asking if she wanted anything to drink, this time she asked for water. She turned back to her book and was so invested in what she was reading that she was surprised when they started to take off. Sarina paused from reading and looked out the window as the plane lifted into the air. *No turning back now, I'm on my way.* On her way to what—she had no idea.

Sarina wasn't sure what to expect when she arrived in Florence, and she still didn't know who was to pick her up at the airport. Her grandmother had taken all the information when Sarina checked in with her while in New York, and her grandmother again just said someone would be there. Sarina pushed her luggage cart to the exit, and she worried that she still had not seen anyone she thought might be there for her. She was beginning to think she had made a mistake and was about to turn around and get on the next plane home when she saw a small sign through the glass doors that led outside. It read, Sarina Forester.

Sarina took a deep breath and pushed the cart outside. As soon as the doors whooshed closed behind her, Sarina heard a gasp and saw three young women talking at once. One of them was holding the name sign. Sarina couldn't understand what they were saying, but by the way they were looking at her and pointing, they had to be talking about her.

Sarina paused, swallowed, and walked over to the women. "Hello. I'm Sarina."

The three young women stopped talking. The one that looked to be the eldest spoke first. "Si—Si, of course you are. You are the very image of our great-grandmother, Gigi."

"Really?" Sarina eyes widened. The whole time growing up she never believed she looked like her mother or her father, so having a resemblance to someone felt good. It surprised her, but it felt good.

"Yes. But where are our manners," said another one of the women. "Hello, dear cousin. And welcome to Italy."

The other two women repeated the same greeting and the three women rushed forward shaking hands and kissing Sarina's cheeks. One of her cousins asked, "Posso ...?" she started, then switched to English. "It's okay?" Pointing to Sarina's luggage, she lifted one of the suitcases.

"Yes, please. I appreciate your help." There was a bustle of four women putting the luggage in the car next to the curb. They all piled in the vehicle after. When the flurry of activity was over, Sarina found herself sitting in the front seat next to the driver. Her heart began to race, and she felt overwhelmed. She looked out the window, not saying much as the driver, her eldest cousin, maneuvered the car into traffic and out of the airport.

Sarina watched out her window when she heard, "I am Sofia," the eldest cousin said. "My sisters in the back are Nicole and Elisa." She motioned toward each of the younger women and looked at Sarina. "Our mother is your mother's sister. Um—was your mother's sister." Sofia's dark eyes grew sad before she looked back at the road. "Um—I'm sorry. I hope I did not upset you."

Sarina waved her hand, as though to dismiss any doubts about what she was about to say. "No, you didn't. Nice to meet you all." Sarina turned to watch the passing sights of the city.

The four women rode in silence for twenty minutes and as they neared the edge of the city Nicole blurted out, "How long will you stay?"

"Nicole!" Sofia snapped.

"It's okay," Sarina said. "I'm not sure actually. It depends."

"Depends on what?" Elisa asked.

Sarina shrugged. "I'm not sure." She paused and thought about the best way to respond. "I guess it depends on how quickly I wear out my welcome." The three other women laughed. They all started talking at once, which caused them all to laugh even louder.

For the next hour, the four women took turns asking questions about each other. How old are you, do you have a boyfriend, are you married, do you have a job? The time passed so quickly that before Sarina knew it, the road crested a hill. Below was a small town nestled against the side of the hill, overlooking the sea.

"Stop!" Sarina yelled.

Sofia jolted, slammed on the brakes, and pulled to the side of the road.

"You okay, Sarina?"

"Yes, I just—please wait a minute." Sarina grabbed her purse and got out of the car. She walked around to stand in the tall grass along the side of the road and stared at the scenery. After a few minutes, Sarina reached into her purse and pulled out the picture of her parents standing in this very spot. Sarina held it up and looked out at the town. A single tear started to fall, and it was as though she could see her young parents standing there laughing while the picture was being taken.

Confused, the three cousins climbed out of the car and joined Sarina.

"Oh! Our mother has that same picture," Nicole exclaimed.

Sarina turned and tried to smile at Nicole, but failed. She realized she must look odd to these strangers. "I'm sorry," she started to apologize.

"No—no," Sofia said. She put her arm around Sarina. "I think I would have done the same thing. This must be strange for you. But you are home now, cousin."

Sarina brightened at the thought of belonging and said, "Thank you." She took one last look. "Okay, I am ready to go."

They piled back into the car and rode in silence the rest of the way. Sofia drove into the town and through the narrow streets. After only a few minutes, she pulled the car onto the side of the road in front of a large stone house. The matching stone and iron gate was currently open. There were flowering plants and bushes and trees poking out of the gate. The cousins jumped out of the car and walked around to the back to help remove Sarina's luggage.

Sarina hesitated and forced herself to get out. She studied her surroundings and tried to take it all in. The scene looked like a postcard.

The road was narrow but wide enough for a car to be parked and another to pass. There was a smattering of stone buildings mashed every which way on either side of the road. Some had gates, some did not. Some had yards, some did not. The road behind her, from where they had come, appeared to snake up the side of the hill with more houses jutting out here and there until the road seemed to disappear.

The road ahead curved slightly and led down the rest of the hillside. It met other roads, and they all coiled like serpents, snaking through the town, and stopping at the edge of the sea. Trees and flowers stuck out like various gems of beauty against the muted tones of stone and iron that made up the buildings, houses, and gates. The view was breathtaking, and Sarina couldn't stop looking at the town nestled below and the bright blue of the sea beyond.

"It's pretty isn't it," Sofia said, her tone matching the awe Sarina felt.

Sarina pulled her gaze from her surroundings and nodded at her cousin. She gathered her purse and one of her carry-on bags. Her cousins insisted on carrying the rest, and Sarina followed Sofia through the gate. Nicole and Elisa followed closely behind.

With every step she took, Sarina's heart pounded faster. It was so loud she thought for sure anyone within a mile could hear it. The butterflies in her stomach were on overdrive and the moisture spread around her collar and under her arms.

Sofia led the way through a tiny flower garden that lined the walkway and up to the front door of the house. Sarina marveled at the beauty around her even though she thought she might throw up. She was dizzy from the contrast of beauty and nerves when Sofia reached the front door. Sofia reached out to open it when the door flew open, followed by shouts in Italian, which Sarina couldn't understand.

Sarina was pulled into the house in a flurry of activity—engulfed in hellos, handshakes, hugs, and kisses on the cheeks. There were greetings in English and Italian, questions all around about her trip and what she thought so far. Sarina looked around and tried to answer each question as best as she could. Her carry-on bag was dropped and forgotten by the front door, but Sarina clutched her purse to her chest as though she were holding on for dear life. Finally, there was a loud noise at the back of the room, and everyone stopped talking at once.

A gray-haired woman, slightly shorter than Sarina, stood in the archway opening which led toward the kitchen. This woman had an air of importance about her, and Sarina couldn't stop staring at her with every step forward she took. Even though she was wrinkled with age, she was a beautiful woman. Her dark eyes twinkled, and there were laugh lines deeply etched around each one.

Sarina gasped when she realized she was looking at an image of what her mother would have eventually looked like if she had lived. The woman held out both her arms as she approached Sarina. "My love. Welcome Home. I am your grandmother, Giada Giacoletti and"—motioning toward an older man sitting in the corner—"that is your grandfather, Cosimo Giacoletti."

The man in the corner stood when his name was mentioned and walked over, stopping in front of Sarina. He had the same dark eyes as Sarina, but his hair was streaked with silver. He had the same laugh lines around his face as her grandmother and his face was equally wrinkled from what Sarina assumed was years of hard work in the sun.

The hush over the room almost unnerved Sarina; it was as though everyone was holding their breath to see if Sarina would be welcomed into the fold. Sarina felt like she should curtsy or bow as the moment seemed to call for it but instead, she looked from one grandparent to the other and thanked them for allowing her to visit.

"Visit? No," her grandfather said. "You are family. This is your home." He paused as though contemplating something. "You should stay."

Sarina grinned. "Yes, thank you, I will stay." *For now.*

The whole room erupted into more chatter and shouting and hugs and laughter. The noise overwhelmed Sarina as she had never been around a large family. Even so, she couldn't help but bask in the warm reception.

As the initial whirlwind died down, the family paused to eat a small luncheon. There was a meat, cheese, and fruit platter, a basket of herbed scones, a large salad, and a loaf of bread, freshly sliced. As the family ate, the wine began to flow. As one of the family members poured Sarina a glass, she was informed that this was the family wine.

"It is magnifico," an uncle said, kissing his fingers and fanning them out.

Sarina laughed, swirled the wine around in the glass, sniffed it, and took a sip. "Magnifico indeed," Sarina exclaimed while everyone laughed at her attempt at saying something in Italian.

Sarina's aunt, who was now pouring the wine, widened her smile. "You know wine?"

"Yes, from a little education from my mother," Sarina explained.

The twinkle in her aunt's eyes disappeared, and her smile turned into a frown. Her aunt turned away so Sarina could no longer see her face. Sarina tried to recall which aunt she was and remembered her as Aunt Gianna. She was her mother's sister and Sarina felt bad for upsetting her, especially after meeting her for the first time. The woman served the rest of the family before she disappeared into the kitchen.

Fearing she'd upset her aunt, Sarina got up and followed her into the kitchen. Her aunt leaned against the sink, whispering. Her eyes were closed and tears ran down her cheeks. Sarina wasn't sure what to say or do, so she made a sound in her throat like she was clearing it. It startled her aunt, but upon seeing Sarina, she smiled.

"I'm okay, dear. I am just sad for my sister."

Sarina nodded. "I am too."

Her aunt rushed to Sarina and held her. She hugged tighter. "Oh, my poor girl."

Sarina sank into the embrace and the two women comforted one another.

A few seconds later her grandmother walked in, made a noise to announce her arrival and said, "Ah, there you are. Come, let's get you settled in your room."

Pulling from her aunt's embrace, Sarina followed her grandmother.

Chapter Five

A noise in the distance caused Sarina to sit straight up in bed. Her hand flew to her pounding heart, and she looked around. Sarina frowned until she remembered where she was. She had been tired from her long journey so had taken a short nap after being shown to her room. She heard the hum of voices below and let out the breath she didn't realize she had been holding. Sarina felt joy wash over her while she thought about these people— her family. Well, her mother's family anyway, and in time she was hoping they would feel like they were her family too.

Swinging her legs over the side of the bed, Sarina stood and walked over to the doors that led to a small balcony. The view was enchanting, and it pulled her outside. She leaned on the railing and took it all in. The sea in the distance sparkled like the sun reflecting off blue glass. The docks were filled with fishing boats and sailing vessels of all shapes and sizes. Shops and cafes were nestled here and there along the street that ran the length of the shoreline. A large circular fountain with graceful figurines rose in the center of the coastal road, with streets veering off from all sides.

More shops and homes lined this area, and Sarina wondered if this was what her mother had referred to once as the village center.

Sarina gazed at the beauty in front of her for a few more minutes, then pulled herself away and walked back into the room. When her grandmother brought her up earlier, Sarina was informed the room had been her mother's as a teenager, and so it was only right that it was now Sarina's.

Sarina looked around at all the details and tried to imagine her mother here. There was a smattering of pictures on the walls—a small, framed painting of some flowers and another of a seascape. The walls were painted a sunny yellow and the curtains that hung from the window and doorway were a stark white in contrast. The quilt on the bed had tiny yellow and blue flowers and the pillowcases and sheets were a pale blue that matched the blue of the flowers in the quilt.

Sarina's bags were stacked neatly against one wall next to a large dresser. She took inventory and confirmed that nothing had been left downstairs in the chaos of her arrival. She noticed the large armoire that stood floor to ceiling and opened one of the doors, checking to see if there would be room to store some of her things out of the way. Sarina made a mental note to ask her grandmother if it was all right to keep her things there. She remembered that the closed door next to the armoire was the small bathroom her grandmother said she could use. She was about to enter it when she heard footsteps outside her bedroom door.

There was a small tap on the bedroom door followed by a muffled voice. "Sarina? You still resting?"

It took Sarina a few seconds to realize it was her aunt. Sarina cleared her throat. "I'm awake now. You can come in."

Aunt Gianna walked in the room. "Are you refreshed?"

"Yes, thank you. I think I'm going to take a quick shower though and change if that's okay."

"Yes, of course."

"Okay, thanks. I shouldn't be too long."

Aunt Gianna paused like she was going to say something else. But appeared to change her mind and turned to leave. "See you downstairs when you are finished."

"Sounds good."

Sarina watched her aunt walk out, shutting the door behind her. She turned back to the chore of washing the grime of travel off her and changing her clothes. She walked into the bathroom and immediately noticed how open the shower was to the rest of the room and was lined with tile, floor to ceiling. The copper pipes were exposed as though plumbing was an afterthought. The sink looked like an old glass bowl with a small copper waterspout hanging over it. It was nestled below a window on a stone platform that jutted out from the wall. To the left of the sink was a small shelf with a mirror resting on it.

The wall opposite the sink held two toilets, and Sarina realized one must be a bidet. The tiled floor sloped gently toward a drain at the back of the room. The copper shower fixtures were intricate, and she fumbled with them until she felt warm water escape from the shower head. She jumped back so as not to get wet and realized she would have to dress in her bedroom since most anything in the room could get damp. Sarina noticed an artisanal looking soap bar, picked it up and breathed in the scent of herbs and lemon. *What a clean smell.* Sarina put the soap bar back in its resting place and went back into her room to undress for her shower.

It didn't take long for Sarina to feel clean again. Once dressed, she pulled her hair back into a braid. Sarina felt a few wisps of hair spring out in defiance, so she glanced in the mirror that hung above the dresser to make sure she was at least presentable. Sarina tried tucking those few pieces of hair back again, but quickly gave up. She left her room and went downstairs.

As she neared the bottom of the staircase it turned slightly, so she was hidden for the moment. As she was about to round the corner, the conversation stopped her. The family was discussing her mother and something about a secret and did Sarina know. They were slipping back and forth from Italian and English, so Sarina only caught bits and pieces, but what she did hear alarmed her. Did Sarina know what happened? Should they tell her what happened? It was her mother's secret and perhaps it should stay in the past. With Sarina in town, the gossip will surely start to flow again. Will anyone in the town say anything to Sarina?

Sarina wondered if this was the terrible truth her mother had spoken off. She thought briefly about running back upstairs and hiding, but decided if she was to make this work, for her mother's sake, she had to face anything that came along. Clearing her throat, Sarina rounded the corner. "Ciao everyone." The entire room stopped talking and exchanged nervous, embarrassed glances.

Sarina's aunt and grandmother bustled into the room with glares for the family and smiles for Sarina. Aunt Gianna said, "Forgive the family's rudeness, Sarina. Come into the kitchen now and have something to eat."

Nodding her head, Sarina followed her aunt out of the room. As the kitchen door was shutting behind her, Sarina could hear both of her grandparents chastising the family and the last thing she heard was her grandmother saying, "Not one more word on the subject!"

Sarina and her aunt exchanged polite smiles while Sarina sat at the kitchen table where a small plate of fruit, cheese, and bread awaited her. There was a tin cup with water, and she drank it. As Sarina ate, she looked around the kitchen, as she hadn't really noticed anything when she had been in the room earlier. She was fascinated by the stone fireplace in the center of one wall. It held a hook where a pot rested, waiting for boiling water. There were the modern amenities such as a small fridge, stove, and kitchen sink. There was also a huge brick oven where a loaf of bread was baking. A mix of the old with the new. Sarina loved it instantly.

Off the kitchen was a back door whose top half was opened to the outside sea breeze that floated into the house. A small porch opened to a veranda surrounded by a stone wall. It overlooked a cliff and the sea beyond. The garden in front extended into the picturesque back garden, and Sarina fell in love with the charm and beauty of it all.

Sarina was finishing her small snack when her aunt sat next to her with a photo album. "I show you pictures, reintroduce you to everyone."

"Oh yes please, that would be wonderful." Sarina laughed. "In the chaos of my arrival I didn't get half of people's names, but don't worry, I do know you are Aunt Gianna."

Aunt and niece shared a laugh as they huddled close and went through each picture slowly.

"This here, of course, is your grandmother Giada—everyone calls her Nonna and you can too—and your grandfather Cosimo Giacoletti," her aunt stated, pointing at the first pictures. "They are the head of the family, outside of my grandmother, your great-grandmother Sara Giacoletti, of course. Your great-grandmother lives at the family vineyard, which you will see tomorrow at the family dinner, along with the cousins who could not be here today."

Aunt Gianna paused, then chuckled. "My grandmother will outlive us all."

"I see." Sarina giggled, staring at the picture and finding her mother's resemblance in them.

As the page turned, Sarina recognized the uncle she'd met briefly in the whirlwind. "Oh, that's Uncle Cosimo Giacoletti—um—the second—named for my grandfather, right?"

"Yes, he is the oldest son and our brother. He is younger than your mother though, as your mother is the oldest. Was the oldest ..." She trailed off, sighed and said, "There was your mom, Luciana, or I think your father called her Lucy. Then, Uncle Cosimo, me—Aunt Gianna and then Uncle Arturo."

Her aunt went on to explain, "Uncle Cosimo the second is married to Aunt Anna and they have two bambinos, a boy, Cosimo the third, and a girl, Silvia. They of course have the family name, Giacoletti." Cosimo the third was not there that day as he helped with the vineyard, but he would be at the family dinner tomorrow. "The rest of that family unit is here today, though."

Sarina listened intently while her aunt pointed at faces, explaining who each person was in every picture.

"I am married to Tomasso De Luca and we have your cousins who brought you, Sofia, Nicole, and Elisa, and we also have two sons, Tito and Alessandro. Alessandro is named for your great-uncle who died a few years back."

Her aunt ran her hand over the pictures as though remembering days gone by. "He was a good man. He was your grandfather Cosimo's brother. Uncle Alessandro has a son who also works at the vineyard,

Alfonso Giacoletti. He is close to my age and he will be at the family dinner too.

Sarina looked at the pictures of her cousins Tito and Alessandro.

Her aunt said, "My boys were sad they missed seeing you today. They own their own restaurant now and needed to work today. They started it a couple years ago and it has been a great success. They will also be at the family dinner."

Another page was turned, and her aunt continued with the introductions. Alessandro was engaged to be married to a girl named Fabiana, but the wedding would wait for a while as he was only twenty-three and the bride-to-be was only twenty. Sofia had a friend named Leone. "But he won't be at the family dinner as they have just begun dating and he is not in the family—yet." She winked as she said the last part.

"Oh," Sarina gasped as the next picture came into view. It was an old picture of Sarina with her mother and father. She was only about four and was laughing at the camera. Her aunt studied the picture with Sarina.

"She was so pretty, my sister," Sarina's aunt said. "And so happy. I am glad, for it meant ..." She trailed off, wiped the tear that slid down her cheek and turned the page, not finishing her thought.

"It meant what?" Sarina asked.

"It's nothing."

More secrets.

"Ah, here is your Uncle Arturo," her aunt said, changing the subject. "He married later in life much to your grandmother's worry and frustration. He married Beatrice from down the road, finally"—this said with a wink—"and they have two boys and two girls who are much younger. Giada, the eldest at thirteen, is of course named for your grandmother and then there is Benedetto who is ten, Sergio is five, and the youngest, Luisa, is three."

"I remember the little ones from earlier," Sarina said. "Just couldn't remember their names."

"You will remember them all in time. We are a big bunch, our famiglia. And you didn't know us until now." She paused as though she wasn't sure she should continue. "I am sorry for that, Sarina."

"Oh—um—well, it isn't your fault, Aunt Gianna."

"I am sorry just the same. Perhaps if things would have been different. But they weren't."

"What things?"

"Life, I guess. But let's not worry about that now," her aunt said, patting her hand. She pulled her hand away, and flipped through more pictures, to introduce more great-aunts and uncles, who were no longer living. Next were second cousins, Leonora, Lorenzo, Basilio and Bianca, who were still living. They lived around town and would be at the family gathering tomorrow. They were the children of Sarina's great-aunts and great-uncles or siblings to her grandfather. Her aunt explained that Sarina's grandfather and only one of his brothers were all that were still alive of the elders. "Except, of course, your great-grandmother. She is nearing ninety and still going strong."

After the last of Gianna's introductions through pictures, she shut the album and handed it to Sarina. "Keep it for now if you like."

Sarina picked up the photo album and thanked her aunt. Nonna shuffled into the room and started to tidy up the kitchen. "The famiglia is beginning to leave for now, Sarina. You should go say your goodbyes."

"Oh yes, of course, Nonna," Sarina said, trying the new name, and went to say her goodbyes. After most had left, Sarina realized her grandfather and her three cousins, Sofia, Nicole, and Elisa were scattered around the room. She sat next to Sofia while they asked a few questions about Sarina getting settled. A few minutes later, Aunt Gianna walked into the living room.

"Okay girls, time to go." The four said goodbye and walked out the front door.

Sarina looked around the room, her gaze landing on her grandfather, and she decided to go sit closer to him. While Sarina was getting settled, Nonna walked into the room and sat next to Sarina. "Now Sarina, tell us about your life."

Sarina paused. *What do I say?* "Well, how much would you like to know? All of it or just bits and pieces?"

"What you want to share is fine."

"Um, I grew up on a farm in the middle of Iowa, which is in the middle of the country. It's usually stifling in the summer and bitter cold in the winter. Mama used to mention she missed the sea breeze when it was hottest, then she would say let's make our own sea so she would pour water into a small wading pool and we would lounge in the water until father came home." Sarina paused, remembering. "After he died, I made her the sea one time to cheer her up. After that, it was a tradition. We made our own sea every year on the first hot day of the year. It became our sign that summer was here."

Sarina realized she was rambling and paused. Her cheeks warmed. "Of course you probably want to know more than just my silly ramblings of a memory about making the sea."

"Your ramblings and memories are fine. You can share those," Nonna said, encouraging Sarina to continue.

"I did fairly well in school. I was going to go to a university a couple hours from home but then Mama got sick, so I went to night school and studied online. I was almost finished before ... well, anyway, I am not yet done with that. I have worked at an accountant's office for several years and since I am majoring in business management and accounting, that job has given me a lot of experience that school can't give me."

Sarina looked from one grandparent to the other as she spoke. "The small town I grew up in, well everyone knows everybody else and everybody's business. But they will have your back if a crisis comes."

"Was it like that for your mama too?" Nonna asked. "She used to tell me she fit in fine, but I sometimes would wonder.

"The town loved Mama. They loved both of my parents, really." Sarina hesitated. "I never seemed to fit though. Not sure why." At this point Sarina stared out the window and said anything that came to mind. It was nice just to talk and have someone really listen and not try to offer words of encouragement or try to make her feel better.

"I remember this one time," Sarina continued, "Mama worked extra hours to buy me a new bike. I loved to ride and the one I had was rusty and falling apart. The chain didn't like to stay on, and the handlebars were almost rusted off. Anyway, she saved and saved. And one day when I got home from school, she took me outside and showed me the surprise. I asked her why I deserved such a gift, and her response was—because you are my sweet daughter."

Sarina smiled at the memory but remembered something else and frowned.

"The day she died I had to work, and I remember being irritated with her as I was running late because she was extra anxious, and she kept asking for the same things over and over again. I felt so awful later when I was called home to say my last goodbye." Tears streamed down Sarina's cheeks. "How horrible am I that I would be irritated with her for such stupid things? I'm glad I made it to her side though."

"You are not horrible, child. She loved you so."

Sarina flinched and looked over at her grandmother. She'd forgotten that anyone else was there and wiped her face. "Thank you. I know she loved me."

"Yes, that she did."

Nonna stood, patted Sarina on the cheek and walked into the kitchen.

The rest of the evening, they talked of more memories. Sarina shared some of her mother as Sarina was growing up and her grandparents shared memories from when her mother was a child. They laughed and talked and sipped the family wine until her grandfather was tired and ready to go to bed. When he left the kitchen, Sarina stood. "I think I will be heading to bed as well."

Before she could leave the room, Nonna gave Sarina pause. "You may hear things at times. Things about your mother. It is best not to pay attention to them." Her grandmother acted as though she was going to say more, but stopped. "Good night, Sarina."

Sarina studied her grandmother. She had so many questions, but decided now was not the time. "Good night, Nonna." Sarina turned and went up to bed.

Chapter Six

Sarina woke to the smell of food and the hum of voices from below. She sat up, stretched, and forced her legs to swing around the side of the bed. She blinked several times, trying to make sense of her surroundings. The past twenty-four hours came rushing back, and that propelled Sarina off the bed and out the door leading to the balcony. She took a deep breath and let the morning sun shine on her face. The sea breeze rushed over her, and she could feel her mouth curve into a wide grin. She forced herself back inside to shower and dress for the day.

She wasn't sure what to expect for the day's activities, so Sarina wore a simple light blue skirt that flowed down to where the hem skimmed her ankles like soft petals. She chose a white T-shirt that she tucked in at her waist, snagged a long scarf that had every shade of blue in it, and tied it around her waist like a belt. She pulled her hair back into a small braid, stopping halfway down the length of her hair. She grabbed a floppy white hat, just in case, and a light sweater, as the breeze appeared to be a little cooler in the morning.

Sarina dug through her suitcase for a smaller purse so that she wouldn't be lugging her big one around all day. Just as she found what she was looking for, she caught a glimpse of the box that contained her mother's urn. She pulled it out of the bag and its container and said, "Well, Mama, we are here." Sarina set the urn on the dresser.

While Sarina was positioning the urn, Nonna knocked softly on the door and poked her head in. "Ah yes, you are up. I thought so." Her grandmother opened the door wider and walked in. "What a beautiful girl."

Sarina laughed. "Thank you!"

The twinkle in her grandmother's eyes faded a bit when she noticed the urn sitting on the dresser.

Sarina picked it up and hugged it close. "I'm sorry. I hope it's okay that I have this here."

Nonna eyed Sarina, then focused on the urn. "She wanted to come home then."

"Yes, she did. This was her dying request that I find a resting place for her here."

The only response Sarina received was a nod. The twinkle flashed back into her grandmother's eyes as quickly as it had vanished. "Well, my daughter and my granddaughter are finally home. One can be happy in that. Come let us go eat, then we will walk about Vetualini a bit."

"That sounds wonderful." Sarina smiled. She replaced the urn on the dresser and followed Nonna down to the kitchen.

About an hour later, Sarina and Nonna left the Giacoletti house and started walking down the road to the area nestled by the sea, which Sarina would learn was the heart of the village. Her grandfather left in his truck headed in the opposite direction. He was going to the Giacoletti vineyard to help prepare for the night's family gathering.

Sarina loved the sights of the houses and the people as they came and went. Most called a greeting to Nonna, which she would always return. After each person was out of earshot, Nonna would turn to Sarina, advise who they were and tell a bit of gossip about them.

This was the game they played all the way down to the fountain Sarina had seen from her window. As they walked around the massive fountain, Sarina noticed an elderly woman all but running toward them. Her arms were flailing about, and she almost dropped her bag of what appeared to be groceries. Nonna stopped walking and said, "Scusami, Sarina." Her grandmother walked to meet the elderly woman.

Sarina wondered about the woman and watched her grandmother engage in a lively conversation in Italian for a few minutes. An approaching boat caught her eye as it neared an empty dock. Sarina turned away from the two women and walked closer to the short stone wall that separated the sea from the road and walkway.

There were two gentlemen with graying beards running about the boat. Sarina loved their gracefulness while they completed the various tasks needed to dock the boat. The two made ready to go ashore and Sarina watched them for a bit longer until she heard a voice say something to her in Italian.

Sarina jumped and turned to find a man standing next to her. She was stunned speechless as she didn't know how long the man had been there. She recovered and said, "I'm sorry I don't speak Italian."

"Ah, it is as I suspect. You are the American Giacoletti cousin."

Sarina studied the man, nodded her head. "Si, I am."

"So, you do speak Italiano."

"Just si."

The man laughed. "Funny and beautiful. It's as it should be."

Sarina laughed. "Do I know you or should I know you?"

"Si, you should know me, or should I say, you should get to know me. Our families know each other

well. Forgive me. I am being rude. I am Antonio
Moretti."

"Nice to meet you. I'm Sarina Forester."

"Hm, well I already knew that."

Sarina's eyebrows raised. "Um—you did? I mean,
how would you know my name?"

"Everyone here knows who you are. At least they
will once you start talking."

They both started to laugh but Sarina heard a
woman calling Antonio's name, looked over his shoulder and said, "You are being called."

"Yes, it is my mother."

"You mustn't keep your mother waiting."

"This is true. She will become more insistent if I
linger."

"They can do that sometimes."

"Yes, mothers, what are we to do?"

Sarina's smiled faded and Antonio ran his fingers
through his hair, looked down at the ground. "Oh my,
I am deeply sorry, Sarina. That was callous of me to
say." Antonio paused, leaned closer and whispered, "I
am sorry for your mother, Sarina."

Sarina smiled a sad smile, thanked him but asked,
"How did you know?"

"Everyone in this town mourned your mother's
passing."

"Oh. I didn't know that." Sarina hesitated. "She was mourned by my hometown as well. She was well-loved everywhere she went, I am finding."

"She was at that. Now I must go." Antonio grabbed Sarina's hand and kissed it lightly, looking at Sarina with a mischievous grin and twinkle in his piercing blue eyes. "Until next time, Sarina."

Smiling, Sarina watched Antonio turn and walk toward his mother. She could see that his mother was asking him a question as he approached, and Sarina knew the moment her son mentioned who she was. His mother's head snapped up and she looked over at Sarina. She studied Sarina, frowned, turned back to Antonio. The woman engaged in a lively conversation with him while the two walked up the road.

Sarina couldn't help but watch mother and son depart. Antonio's dark head was turned slightly down toward his mother, and even though she seemed to be frowning, Antonio still had a handsome smile. His tanned complexion made it seem he spent a lot of time in the sun. As though he could feel Sarina watching him, he turned his head toward her, flashed her another mischievous grin, and waved.

Sarina grew hot from head to toe at being caught staring at Antonio. Her heart beat a little faster at their exchange, and her hand still felt warm where

Antonio had held it. She smiled and waved at the departing Antonio as her grandmother walked up beside her.

"Ah, yes," Nonna said, "Antonio." She paused, watched the mother and son, and turned to Sarina. "He grew to be a handsome boy. He is about your age. Perhaps a year or two older."

She seemed to study Sarina. "He is the very image of his father, most will say, but I see a lot of his mother in him. Our families almost joined together but we didn't, and things turned out as they should."

Sarina prayed her grandmother couldn't see her reaction to Antonio and she didn't have to wait long for an answer.

Nonna laughed. "Don't fret, my girl. You are not the first woman to be caught staring after a handsome man. At least you were not drooling and slack jawed." She laughed even harder, and Sarina looked down at the ground. She decided not to let the teasing get to her and soon joined in the laughter.

Nonna linked her arm with Sarina. "Come, let's go see your cousins' restaurant and get something to eat."

Two hours later, Sarina was finishing the meal cooked especially by her cousin Alessandro, and she couldn't eat another bite if she tried. He'd made her a beet risotto with truffle oil and an open-faced beef carpaccio sandwich. She had water and a glass of Villa di Giacoletti Sangiovese to wash it down. Sarina enjoyed the flavor meld of the beef and risotto with the fruity, spice, and oak flavors of the wine her family was known for.

Alessandro and Tito took turns talking and visiting with their cousin and grandmother while the other ran the restaurant. But it was Alessandro and Sarina who seemed to really hit it off. Sarina realized it was the same connection she felt with Sofia.

Sarina could tell that the brothers were close as they worked and talked and visited. She wondered what it would have been like if her mother had not miscarried her baby brother, causing complications which prevented her from having more children. Perhaps her life would have been different. Perhaps she would be sitting here taunting a younger brother and the two of them would be on this journey together. But to wish it wouldn't make it happen, so Sarina forced all thoughts of the "what ifs" aside and focused on the family who was here, and her surroundings.

The rustic décor of the restaurant gave it a traditional Italian flare. It served Italian food but would prepare a few American dishes for those tourists who wanted a taste of home. The bar was large, made of solid wood, with a shiny yet natural finish. Behind the bar, glass shelves housed various liquors. Along one section of the wall was a large wine rack with various wine glasses hanging down from the bottom.

Sarina admired the décor and the feel of the place as she looked around, while Alessandro shared stories of his youth. She laughed often and would join in with stories of her own crazy antics as a child. Sarina noticed her grandmother just sat back and watched. Nonna seemed to be enjoying the stories, but Sarina wondered if her grandmother enjoyed watching her grandchildren becoming friends, more.

When the two women finished their meals and Tito mentioned for the third time that it was starting to get busy and he could use Alessandro's help, Sarina and her grandmother finally stood and said their goodbyes with promises to see them later that evening at the family dinner.

As Sarina walked out of her cousins' restaurant, Alessandro and Tito called a final farewell. Sarina turned slightly to respond and as she turned back around, she slammed into the side of a man who was walking outside the restaurant door. Sarina almost fell to the ground, but caught herself by grabbing the man's arm and pulled herself up.

By the time Sarina was steady, the man was red faced and screaming at her in Italian. Sarina tried to apologize over and over, to no avail. When the man finally stopped his tirade, Sarina looked at him and tried to apologize once again.

"You have nothing to say to me that I want to hear, you American trash," he shouted at Sarina.

Sarina stumbled backwards at his insults but still tried to stammer out an apology.

"Aldo Bianchi, you will not talk to my granddaughter that way," Nonna yelled from behind her.

"The sins of the dead mother should be paid by the living daughter. One born of trash will always be trash."

"Aldo! Perhaps the sins of the dead son should be paid by the living father then."

"Aach." The man threw up his arms, spit on the ground next to Sarina's feet, and rushed past her. He stomped the rest of the way down the sidewalk.

Shaken by what the stranger said, Sarina thought about the words her mother had written. Sarina was certain that whatever the secret was, it was something awful. Sarina had been feeling indifferent about finding out the details, but this encounter changed that. She resolved to learn everything.

Nonna wrapped her arm around Sarina as her cousins came running outside. Tito called after the retreating man, saying, "You will not be welcome in our restaurant any longer, Aldo Bianchi."

The man didn't turn around, but Sarina could hear him say something in Italian as he rounded the corner and disappeared out of sight.

Chapter Seven

So, you had interesting day," Sarina's grandfather said as he maneuvered the car up the hill on the way out of town.

Sarina, who was sitting in the back seat, glanced at her grandfather's reflection in the rear-view mirror and smiled. "You could say it was interesting."

"Don't pay any attention to that old buffoon, Aldo. He is just sore over his son's death and"—clearing his throat—"blames—"

"Cosimo!" Nonna shouted, startling Sarina and her grandfather. "Watch the road."

Sarina's grandfather said something in Italian to which her grandmother replied. They carried on for a few minutes and it sounded to her like they were arguing.

Her grandmother glanced at Sarina and smiled sweetly. "Let's talk of something else."

"Yes," Sarina's grandfather said and winked at Sarina in the mirror.

Sarina tried not to think about the exchange as she watched the Italian countryside out her window, but she couldn't help but wonder what her family was keeping from her.

"It won't take much longer, Sarina," her grand-father said as he turned right on a road a little past the village limits. "It is only about a fifteen-minute drive once you reach the edge of town."

Sarina watched the passing landscape. She found her surroundings beautiful, but her thoughts contin-ued to stray to her mother's secret. It didn't take long before the car slowed down. Sarina pulled herself out of her trance as her grandfather said, "There it is."

Sarina turned her gaze from the countryside and looked straight ahead. She saw a tall brick wall stretching right and left, with a large iron gate in the center. It was open now, and Sarina's grandfather drove the car through it and up a tree-lined driveway that led to a stone villa. It was two stories, with a large Juliet balcony overlooking the front. Floor to ceiling windows covered the entire wall on either side of the balcony and a large stone patio nestled below the rounded front doorway.

Sarina looked around and marveled at the gran-deur of the place. She had originally thought the family vineyard was more of a hobby, but seeing the magnitude of what was in front of her, she realized it must be much more.

Instead of driving to the front of the villa, Sarina's grandfather followed a narrow drive that continued past the right side of the villa. He pulled to a stop, and

Sarina gasped at the view as she climbed out of the backseat. The villa rested above vast rolling hills of grapevines. There was a large stone barn-like structure down the hill and to the right, plus several other smaller stone buildings scattered about, which added to the beauty of the landscape.

Directly off the back of the villa was a large courtyard with a pergola covering half of it. The pergola held vines with purple flowers and soft twinkling lights. Below the center of the pergola was an extralong table that appeared to have had years of use, with benches and chairs of various shapes and sizes nestled under it. Leading out from the courtyard was a small path that ran into a stoned circular area. It had a fire pit in the center, and more benches and chairs sprinkled around it.

The path continued past the fire pit but veered toward the left before stopping at a massive vegetable garden. It picked up beyond the vegetable garden and ran through a beautiful flower garden, with benches randomly placed. And everywhere in the landscape, Sarina saw numerous old trees rising to meet the deep blue sky.

Sarina couldn't help but stare at her surroundings. *This beautiful place puts my little farm in Neely to shame.* Sarina chastised herself for thinking poorly of her home and followed her grandparents into the villa through a side door next to where they had parked.

Once inside she was immersed in the same loud chaos of greetings as when she had first arrived the day before. In between greetings and hugs and pecks on the cheek Sarina looked around the room. It was a living space big enough to hold her family and more. Couches and chairs were strewn about, and a fireplace adorned one wall.

The archway on the other side of the room took up over half the wall and it led into an open foyer. The floors were made of various sized stones, and they held a smattering of rugs. On the other side of the foyer, Sarina noticed a doorway leading into a room full of bookshelves, and to the right of that doorway was a massive staircase that curved around to the right. Sarina itched to see more of the grand house, but instead she focused on greeting her family.

After greetings and warm welcomes and assurances that Sarina's first day in Italy was a good one, the family broke into small groups. Loud conversations continued all around. Sarina was talking with Sofia, Elisa, and Aunt Gianna when the room suddenly became quiet. Sarina turned her head and saw the matriarch of the family, and her great-grandmother, Sara Giacoletti. She stood below the archway and looked around the room as though she were searching for something or someone. Her gaze landed on Sarina and with a deliberate gait, she didn't waver in her path straight for Sarina.

Sarina wasn't sure what she expected when meeting her great-grandmother, but it was not this force walking toward her. Her great-grandmother's strength emanated from her with every step forward, but she still had a gracefulness about her.

Her great-grandmother stopped short, and Sarina wasn't sure if she should bow or hug the woman who stood in front of her. Her great-grandmother answered that question by pulling Sarina into a warm embrace. When they pulled apart, Sarina was startled to find herself staring into her own eyes, as though looking in a mirror at her future self.

Her great-grandmother laughed. "It is like looking in a mirror and seeing my younger self. She is a true Giacoletti through and through."

A sense of belonging washed over Sarina and she laughed along with the older woman while those around her nodded their agreement or joined the laughter. Sarina's great-grandmother pulled her over to a small love seat to sit together. "Now let's visit while wine is served to everyone." There was a small flurry of activity as wine bottles and glasses were passed around. Sarina noted there were several bottles of the same sangiovese she had at lunch, plus there were several bottles of the family's pinot grigio.

The two women regarded each other while the wine was passed. Sarina's great-grandmother broke the silence. "So, you are named for me, no?"

"Yes, that is partly true," Sarina said. "I am named for both you and my father's mother. They tried to combine Sara, which is from you, of course, and Renee, which was my Grandma Forester's name. My mother was originally going to spell it S-a-r-e-n-a-e. But my father was afraid that people would mispronounce it, so he requested that it be Sarina."

"Si—si." Sarina's great-grandmother nodded, appeared to study Sarina, and changed the subject by asking, "Was she in pain in the end?"

Sarina flinched from the unexpected question and almost spilled her wine, but she recovered quickly. "No, she seemed to be at peace. She was ready to go."

Her great-grandmother nodded and said, "It's as it should be, no?"

Sarina's face softened and she nodded. Wanting to change the subject, she said, "Your home is beautiful. I have never seen anything like it."

"But this is your home too, my child," her great-grandmother said with a quizzical look at Sarina. "Just as it was your mother's before you."

Sarina's cheeks grew warm. "Oh well, thank you."

"Perhaps we should walk about. I will show you the place."

"That sounds great."

They stood, and Sarina followed her out into the foyer and was shown around the house. The stairs led to a large landing with several hallways running off it. The bookshelves she'd seen earlier were part of a library, which led to an office. Sarina was shown the kitchen, dining room, a great room, and another office before being led upstairs on a back staircase off the kitchen.

Her great-grandmother talked about how the villa was built by Sarina's great-grandfather's ancestors and the house, the property, and vines passed from first born to first born since the first Giacoletti bought the land. The vineyard had grown from a small hobby to a good and profitable business. "Everyone in the family has worked at the villa at one time or another if they don't currently work here now," she explained.

"My first born is your grandfather," her great-grandmother went on to explain. "But though he has a love for the vineyard and continues to work with the vines occasionally, his true love is tending to the animals and puttering around the gardens"—with a look of pride—"he is much like his father."

"So, my great-grandfather loved that part of the work too?" Sarina asked.

"Yes," her great-grandmother said. "Over the years your great-grandfather willingly turned the day to day running of the vineyard to me and he focused on the grounds and animals. He had a passion for goat cheese and making different cheeses with the goat's milk, which we sell."

Sarina followed her great-grandmother down a long hallway while the woman chattered on. "Your grandfather focuses most of his work on that part of the estate, while me and some of the others help with the day-to-day operation of the vineyard. Alfonso, Cosimo the third, and Sofia are the great-grandchildren who help. Although at harvest everyone in the family pitches in with something." Her great-grandmother finished as the two walked into an oversized bedroom.

What a sunny room.

The walls were painted a pale yellow, much the same shade as the room she was staying in at her grandmother's house. On one wall white stripes provided an accent, and the center of that wall housed a beautiful painting of the vineyard. Below it was a large chair that one could curl up in to read or to take a nap. The bed was in the center of the opposite wall with a large window and window seat on one side and

French doors on the other, leading out to a balcony that overlooked the picturesque grounds below.

Sarina peeked out and noticed that a lot of the rooms on this side of the house had small balconies. This room was almost center of the back of the house, save one. Sarina turned her focus back to the interior and as she surveyed it, she caught her great-grandmother staring at her with a questioning glint in her eye. Sarina realized that her great-grandmother had grown quiet when they had entered the room.

"Great-grandmother, I ..."

"Please child, call me Gigi. It is what famiglia call me," her great-grandmother interrupted.

Sarina felt another wave of belonging wash over her. "Okay—Gigi—I love how the armoire, dresser, and dressing table are slightly different pieces of furniture, but they all still seem to match," Sarina said motioning in their direction.

"Do you like the desk?" her great-grandmother asked.

"Yes, it is very pretty," Sarina responded. "It blends in nicely with the rest of the room's furnishings." Sarina felt strange talking so much about this room, especially since this was the longest time they had spent anywhere on the tour.

"Go and check out the bathroom." Her great-grandmother motioned toward a closed door.

Sarina walked over and looked in. It was much bigger than Sarina thought it would be. It held a beautiful bathtub under a window, a stand-alone shower which was open to the room, a sink, a toilet, and a bidet. Sarina realized that even though this home was built several centuries ago, it was very much updated.

"You like the room?" Gigi asked when Sarina turned around.

"Yes, it's a beautiful room."

"This is wonderful," Gigi responded. "This was your mother's room, and it is now yours for when you stay here."

Sarina's mouth dropped open. She paused and gestured so as to encompass the room. "I can't take this room. What about the rest of the family?"

"Ah, it warms my heart that you think of them. Those who are interested in the family business have their own rooms. But you, my dear girl, are the rightful heir to this entire estate so naturally you should get one of the best rooms."

Sarina felt the blood drain from her face, and became dizzy. "What—I mean—are you sure you mean me? That can't be right."

"Sarina, you are the first born, of the first born, of the first born."

"I ..." Sarina paused, wanting to sit. "I don't know what to say."

"Say nothing for now." Gigi paused and appeared to be contemplating how to explain. "If you wish to learn more, you can stay. If you wish to return with my son and daughter-in-law and stay with them, you may. It is your choice. But this will always be here waiting for you."

Still not sure how to respond, Sarina turned and walked toward the French doors, paused, and stared out at the vast grounds. "May I take some time to think about it?"

"Of course." Gigi's expression brightened. "I know in my heart you will be the perfect one to pass the estate to, but you need to figure this out for yourself, Sarina. Take all the time you need."

The two women made their way back through the house and joined the others. As they entered the living area, a young woman walked in saying something in Italian, which Sarina quickly figured out meant dinner was ready. The family filed out to the courtyard and scattered around the table, which held various Italian dishes. Sarina smiled at the beautiful arrangements of flowers, candles, water glasses and wine goblets. It was a grand display, in contrast to the rustic wood. And Sarina loved every bit of it.

I could get used to this. Sarina cleared her throat as though to push that thought aside and joined the group of strangers who she had to remind herself was her family, and found a seat. Sarina tried to concentrate on the conversation at the table, joined in the laughter, and shared stories when asked to participate. However, the conversation she had with her great-grandmother a short time ago lingered in the back of her mind.

It was thinking of that very conversation that caused Sarina to glance over at her great-grandmother. Gigi was talking to a cousin, but it was like she felt Sarina looking at her because she paused her conversation, looked at Sarina and smiled. Sarina couldn't help but smile back, then turned to Nicole, who was sitting next to her to answer a question.

The dinner went well, and Sarina had a nice visit with the family who sat around her. And even though they still felt like strangers to her, she started to feel more comfortable and would join in the banter toward one cousin or another. However, one of her cousins seemed a bit reserved toward her—her older second cousin, Alfonso. He greeted her and was polite when introduced, but he seemed to study Sarina as though she were an intruder rather than a family member. Sarina decided it was best to steer clear of him. She didn't want to cause friction in the family. After all, she *was* the outsider.

After dinner was completed and the dishes were cleaned, the family took their drinks of choice and gathered around the fire pit. A few of the cousins could play the guitar or violin, so there was music with the fire.

Sarina listened intently and observed the entire group, trying to take it all in. A few of the family members drifted away from the fire at times but they would return usually with more wine in hand. Nonna left the circle at one point and when she came back, she sat next to Sarina.

"Ah, my love. How are you doing?"

"I'm doing well," Sarina responded. "The food and the family—well—it's all been so wonderful. A bit overwhelming at times, but in a good way."

"Si. We have that effect on people."

The two laughed. Nonna quieted and said, "So you have been told what you can do."

Sarina almost spilled her drink. "Um—yes. But how did you know?"

"It is my job to always know what is happening with my children and even my grandchildren. Besides that, you are the first born of a first born of a first born."

"That is what Gigi said."

"Yes, it is as it should be. You to be here."

Sarina stared into the fire contemplating what she should do. "I wasn't sure if I should stay here or not. I don't want to take away the time with you."

"No, and you won't by being here. Your grandfather and I want the best for you. And this place, your heritage, this is best for you."

"How can you be sure I am best for it though?"

"Ah, see that is the question you must answer for yourself. But the only way to get that answer is to remain here. You can come home with us tonight if you want. But if you decide, we can bring you back in the morning along with your things. It is important for you to learn about this as it is a part of who you are."

"I guess I don't understand how it's a part of who I am when Mama never even told me about this place."

Her grandmother frowned as she reached out her hand and placed it over Sarina's. "Your mama wanted this for you, or she would not have sent you here." Nonna took a deep breath. "And your mama, she—ran from this place, but I believe she always meant to return some day—with you. And so, she did, I guess, but I expect a bit differently than what she envisioned."

Sarina turned toward the fire and studied it for a long time before turning back to her grandmother. "Okay, I will give it a try. Tomorrow we can come back, and I will see what I can do."

"Excellent. I will inform Mama that you will be coming."

Nonna got up to go tell Gigi the news when from across the fire Nicole called out, "So Sarina, I heard you met the handsome Antonio today." Nicole and a few others burst into laughter, teasing Sarina.

Sofia said, "So, what do you think of this handsome Italian man?" The two sisters broke into laughter again while Sarina felt her face grow hot. She hoped the fire light hid her flamed cheeks.

Sarina cleared her throat. "He was nice enough."

"Yes, well he was quite taken with you," this from Elisa. Suddenly Nonna started saying something in Italian and Sarina could tell by her cousins' chagrined looks that they were being chastised.

Sarina turned to her grandmother and said, "It's okay."

"Well, we shall see," Nonna said.

The conversation turned to the vineyard and the following day's activities and responsibilities. Some of the family stayed and participated, while others started to drift back toward the villa. Sarina looked across the fire where Alfonso was glaring at her. She grew uncomfortable under his gaze and wondered what she did to upset him.

"Come, Cosimo. Come, Sarina. We must be going. Early morning tomorrow." It was her grandmother's direction to go that seemed to encourage everyone else to leave as well. The family said their goodbyes, and more hugs and pecks on the cheeks were passed around. Sarina told Gigi she would be returning in the morning. She turned and was off with her grandparents back to town.

Chapter Eight

Sarina had been at the villa for several days and was amazed at how fast time had gone by. She had been in Italy for almost a week and the longer she was there, the more at home she felt. She kept on her guard because she had not made up her mind if she wanted to stay or go home to Iowa. Of course, she thought, she was probably the only person in the world who was given such an opportunity and yet kept Iowa in her back pocket. But Sarina had reservations and believed they stemmed from the giant dark secret regarding her mother. And it loomed over her head most of the time.

Sarina was sitting outside in the flower garden leaning against a tree sipping coffee while contemplating all of this, when she heard someone approaching. She turned, half expecting to see one of her cousins or Gigi, and flinched, almost dropping her coffee. A stream of dark liquid slid over the cup's rim and burned her finger. "Ouch," she exclaimed. Sarina felt like an idiot as she fumbled with her mug, so she set it on the grass next to her. She looked back over at the approaching figure, feeling her cheeks flame. "Hello, Antonio."

Antonio slowed his pace. "I'm sorry, I didn't mean to frighten you," he said with the same twinkle in his eyes as before and the same devilish grin on his face.

"Somehow I don't believe you," Sarina said as she studied the man in front of her. The mischievous curve of his lips and laughing eyes gave a different story from remorse.

"Well, perhaps I can make it up to you."

Sarina rolled her eyes. "That won't be necessary. But thank you."

Antonio's smile widened. "Putting up barriers I see."

"I don't know what you're talking about, but I would like to finish my coffee in peace. And what are you doing here anyway?"

"Your great-grandmother is my employer. I work here."

"You work here at the vineyard?"

"Si."

"Why have I not seen you here before?"

"I don't know. Perhaps because I have been in the vines mostly." Antonio went on to explain more. "My papa needed to discuss a few things with your great-grandmother, so we rode here together today, and he dropped me at the front."

"I see."

"You should go meet him. He is interested in meeting you."

Sarina's eyebrows raised. "Why is that?"

Antonio studied Sarina and she wondered what he was thinking before he said, "So you don't know then."

"Don't know what?" Sarina asked.

"It is not my place to say." Antonio fidgeted. "Excuse me now, I must get to work. Have a good day la mia bella amica."

"Um, you too," Sarina said, puzzled by what he said. She thought *mia* meant my and *amica* meant friend but wasn't sure what the rest of the phrase meant. She made a mental note to ask Sofia about it later.

Sarina watched Antonio walk past her, toward the back of the gardens and on to the vineyard. As he started to walk in between the vines, he turned, flashed a wide grin, waved at Sarina, and disappeared into the vines. Her cheeks burned again because she had been caught staring after him a second time and she hated that he'd caught her, again. Sarina turned her gaze from the vineyards and thought she heard laughter coming from the vines and rolled her eyes, thinking he must be laughing at her. "Oh," Sarina huffed out, picked up her mug, and made her way back to the villa.

Sarina deposited her coffee mug into the sink once inside the kitchen. She strolled down the hall into the office where she heard Gigi talking. She was supposed to meet with her in about ten minutes anyway, so decided to head there now. As Sarina poked her head into the office, she noticed an older version of Antonio. He was sitting in a chair on the other side of the desk, across from her great-grandmother.

"Oh, I'm sorry," Sarina said. "I will come back."

"No, please come in, Sarina," Gigi said, stopping Sarina from leaving. "There is someone here I would like for you to meet."

Sarina nodded at Gigi, opened the door further and walked into the office. Sarina smiled at her great-grandmother fondly, as she and the man stood.

"Sarina, I would like for you to meet Stefano Moretti. He is Antonio's father."

Sarina smiled, held out her hand to shake his. "Hello."

Antonio's father took her hand in both of his. "It is so wonderful to meet you, Sarina." He studied her closely as though he were trying to find something. "She has the look of you, Sara, and not Luc. This is a bit surprising, no?"

"Yes, Stefano. I was surprised as well," Gigi agreed.

Sarina continued smiling, nodding her head as though she agreed and tried to keep her cheeks from flaming red from the scrutiny. Sarina was not used to so much attention, and this close study of her made her nervous.

"She has Luc's sparkle, though doesn't she?" Stefano continued. He let go of Sarina's hand but continued his study of her.

"Si, she does at that," Gigi said.

"Si—Si." Changing the subject, Stefano said, "So you have met my boy, Antonio. He is a good boy but needs a strong one to keep his feet on the ground." Stefano burst out laughing and said, "It is a good thing he works here. It teaches him things he needs to learn."

"We try, Stefano, we do try," Gigi said and joined the laughter as though it were an inside joke.

Sarina's great-grandmother stopped laughing but was still smiling when she said, "Come Stefano, I walk you out. Sarina, you may remain here for our meeting. I will return momentarily."

"Oh well, Gigi, I can walk him out," Sarina suddenly blurted out. She could tell her great-grandmother was tired today so Sarina wanted to help however she could, even if it was a simple task, like walking a guest to the door. Gigi nodded her approval and said her goodbyes. Sarina and Stefano walked out of the office toward the front door.

Stefano stopped short of the front door. "I must know, did she have pain in the end?"

Sarina winced at the question. "No." Sarina sighed, then frowned. "I mean—um—I'm sorry I didn't mean to respond so abruptly."

"No, it's okay, Sarina. I surprised you, I can tell."

Sarina studied Stefano, and felt she had to be gentle in her response. "No, she didn't suffer in the end. She was at peace." Sarina's lower lip quivered, and she struggled to keep her composure. "I'm sorry," Sarina mumbled as she turned toward the front door.

"You miss her."

Sarina's shoulders slumped forward. "Every day, all the time, every breath I take."

"I know how that feels, Sarina," Stefano said, "and I wish I could say it will go away but you will always miss her. But how you deal with it will get easier."

"How do you know?" Sarina managed to ask.

"Because I too miss her every day, all the time, and with every breath I take, and I have missed her this way ever since she left so long ago."

"I don't understand," Sarina blurted out at Stefano's confession.

"I suppose you wouldn't."

Sarina remembered what her grandmother had said a few days before about the two families almost being joined together. "You and my mother were close?"

"Very close."

"What happened?"

"That is a story for another day, Sarina."

Sarina remembered the woman walking with Antonio the other day, his mother. Sarina frowned. "You married someone else."

"Yes. Her name is Valentina. She was your mother's closest friend growing up, and she knows the love I have for Luc, but the heart has room for a lot of love in life, Sarina. You must come and meet Valentina. She wants to meet you."

"I will try," she said softly. Stefano left then, and a puzzled Sarina walked back into the office where her great-grandmother was waiting.

Gigi was writing in one of the ledgers when Sarina walked in. When her great-grandmother saw the expression on her face, she set the pen down. "Are you okay, Sarina?"

"I'm okay. But I am confused about things that happened with my mother before she left."

"I see."

"Everyone appears to love her and miss her," Sarina said. "But I can't help but get the feeling that she left under circumstances that were not the greatest, which in some ways hurts, because then I wonder if she really loved my father."

Gigi had a guarded expression when she said, "Sarina, your mother loved your father very much. What tore Stefano and Luciana apart happened long before your mother left, and it was your father that helped to heal her heart. She chose to make a life with him in Iowa because she loved him."

"Yes, but I'm beginning to believe that there is more to it than that, especially after the letter she wrote me," Sarina explained.

"What letter?" Gigi asked as she stood.

Sarina stepped closer to the desk. "I found it in her keepsake box. She told me that she hoped I would forgive her and still love her after I found out something. But I don't know what she is talking about and I am beginning to think everyone here knows what that is but me."

Her great-grandmother frowned. "Well, Sarina, that is part of the problem. No one really knows what happened, no one still living anyway, so it is hard to say."

Sarina studied Gigi, trying to figure out what to ask. "Can you at least tell me what you and everyone else know?"

"Yes, but I would like for us to do that sometime later." Gigi walked around her desk and put her arm around Sarina. "You are upset right now ... and besides, we have work to do."

Frustration grew inside Sarina, but she didn't want to push the subject, so chose to drop it. She respected her great-grandmother too much. "Okay, let's get to work."

The two women walked around the desk and huddled together, looking over the ledgers for the next couple of hours. They discussed the different markings and what they meant. Gigi explained the calculations and the reasoning behind some of the decisions made. Sarina listened intently, but as she caught on to the markings and entries, she noticed something that looked odd. She asked her great-grandmother about it, but Gigi wasn't sure about it either. Sarina asked if it would be okay to go over all the books.

"Yes, please do," Gigi responded. "My son, your great-uncle Alessandro, used to handle the accounting, but he had a heart attack several years ago and passed away, which is when Alfonso took over. Alfonso had been working with his father, so it made sense. It was a fairly easy transition."

Sarina wondered about the transition and asked, "Does anyone else study the books or work on them?"

"My other son, your great-uncle Tobia, works on them occasionally, but he has been going through a difficult time of it since his wife passed. He pretty much lets Alfonso handle everything," Gigi explained.

Hmm, I wonder ...

Gigi appeared to be studying Sarina before she asked, "Do you not believe this is a good thing?"

"Oh, I don't know really. I'm sure it's okay," Sarina tried to reassure. "After all he is a Giacoletti. I'm sure it's nothing and just a misunderstanding on my part."

"Yes." Gigi's expression warmed but she continued to study Sarina intently.

Gigi gave all the records and ledgers to her. Sarina noted that they went as far back as when her mother had been working at the villa. Sarina said, "I probably don't need to go back that far, but it's a good place to start I guess."

Chapter Nine

Sarina pored over one of the ledgers while she sat at a makeshift desk in the wine barn. She made a mental note of when things started to be moved to a computer program, but parts of the accounting were still in the original format in ledger books. Due to the different formats, studying everything would be more difficult, but she was confident that with her knowledge of accounting, she would be able to figure it out in no time.

She was double checking some of the definitions and markings with what was currently in the barn, to make sure she knew what she was looking at. She was about to finish that task for the day when Alfonso walked in. He stopped short and stood so his shadow covered the pages of the ledger.

Sarina's eyebrows creased and she looked up. Her frown changed to a smile. "Oh, hello Alfonso."

Alfonso scowled "What are you doing, Sarina?"

Sarina believed she should tread carefully with Alfonso. "I'm just trying to learn about the vineyard. I am a Giacoletti so I should know what it means to be a Giacoletti, right?" Sarina chuckled trying to lighten the atmosphere, but the only response she got was a half-smile that looked more like a sneer.

Alfonso studied her with a guarded look and said, "Maybe." He sighed, ran his fingers through his hair. "Look, I am sure you probably can tell I am a little— unsure about you being here. It is difficult to have someone from the outside poke around the famiglia business."

Sarina understood now. He was protective of the family.

"I see." Sarina tried to reassure her older cousin by saying, "Alfonso, I assure you, I'm not here to hurt anyone or step on toes or take anything away from anyone that belongs to them. You are all the family I have left, so I'm trying to learn about you all and what you do."

Alfonso's expression brightened. "Well, I guess if you say. It might be kind of nice to have some help with all the ledgers. It is kind of a mess transferring it all to electronic."

"I can imagine. I'm happy to help anyway that I can."

"I appreciate that." Alfonso looked over at the wine barrels, then back at Sarina as though making up his mind about something and said, "Maybe I use your help." He smiled widely. "Some men are coming to see the vineyard. They are businessmen that—eh—um—

are going to model Italian vineyard and villa to create oasis for vacationers and they are visiting several for—um—research. Perhaps it would be nice for you to join me. They speak English and I am not always able to understand them."

Sarina grinned. She felt like she conquered a small battle of winning over her cousin. "Of course. I would love to help."

"Great. Okay. They will be here next Wednesday morning at nine. Let's meet in front of the wine barn."

"I'll be here," Sarina said still smiling.

Alfonso nodded, and walked away.

Feeling pleased with herself, Sarina decided to be done with her work for the day. She gathered the ledgers and walked out of the barn, where she ran right into a solid object that let out a loud "Ooof."

Sarina stumbled back. "Oh, for the love of ..." She trailed off and cleared her throat. "What are you doing here, Antonio?"

He looked down at her and laughed. "You are so pretty when you are flustered."

Sarina couldn't help but smile. "Well, you tend to always see me at my worst."

"No, not worst."

Rolling her eyes, Sarina mumbled a goodbye. But as she walked past him, Antonio snagged her arm, swung her around, and held her close. He studied her with a guarded expression, and she thought he might kiss her. Instead, he said, "Sometimes I can't tell if you are annoyed with me or making fun of me."

Sarina felt something—frustration—desire—rise inside her, which she was sure Antonio didn't miss. He looked like he was bracing himself for a verbal beating, but Sarina bit her tongue and he relaxed. She was annoyed and wanted to yell at him about man handling her, causing her to spill coffee, and laughing at her, but she decided to take the high road. She did yank her arm free though and said, "I do not require your assistance in walking, sir, so I would be happy if you did not grab my arm."

Antonio flashed his teeth. "Perhaps one of these days you and I can actually have a conversation and get to know one another better without the interference of duties calling."

Sarina's only response was the lift of one eyebrow. Antonio's face displayed a range of emotions.

After an awkward silence between them, Sarina finally turned, called a farewell to Antonio, and started to walk away.

"Until we meet again, la mia bella amica," Antonio responded.

I really need to ask Sofia what that phrase means. Sarina lifted her hand over her head, attempting a half wave, and kept walking.

Antonio's laughter bubbled up and she felt his eyes watching her. Sarina giggled, started to round a curve in the path, but paused and turned with a goofy grin. She confirmed Antonio was watching her, waved, laughed harder, turned, and ran out of sight.

Sarina thought she heard Antonio say, "I'm in big trouble." But she pushed all thoughts of what that could mean out of her mind.

Chapter Ten

The following Wednesday dawned with sunlight pouring into Sarina's room. She had been up for several hours poring over the ledgers. She had already grasped all the little notes and symbols and where the vineyard was at financially.

There was still something troubling her about the books and she wanted to ask Great-uncle Tobia about it. Glancing at the clock, she realized it would have to wait. Sarina needed to get ready for the day and the meeting with Alfonso and the businessmen who were arriving in a few hours. Sarina hurried to dress, picking something she thought to be suitable and was about to pull her shoes out from the armoire when there was a knock on the door.

"Come in," Sarina called.

The door cracked slightly, then Gigi's foot shoved it open with a loud thud before she shuffled into the room. She carried a tray filled with coffee, fruit, and bread. Sarina rushed over to help her great-grandmother, who waved her off. Gigi walked over to the desk where Sarina had been working and set the tray on top of it. She turned, greeted Sarina and said, "Sit, eat, let's talk awhile."

Sarina was puzzled but obeyed. She had eaten half of her food in silence when Gigi asked, "So, you like it here so far, no?"

Sarina brightened. "I've really enjoyed my time here, yes."

"Very good. I am happy to hear this. Perhaps you should consider staying in Italy and not going back to Iowa?"

Sarina stopped the grape halfway to her mouth. She put it back on the plate and studied her great-grandmother. Struggling with how to respond, she looked around the room, then looked out the window. As Sarina studied the view, she contemplated her great-grandmother's question.

Silence filled the room.

Sarina turned back to Gigi and took a deep breath. "There is no denying that I am falling in love with this place," Sarina started, "but I still need some time to think about it. I do have a farm back home that was left in my keeping and I can't in good conscience just abandon it."

"A wise girl you are, Sarina. I thought you would say this."

"Really?"

"Yes, you are so much like your mother and so very much like me."

Sarina's eyebrows rose and her mouth dropped open. "I never thought I was like Mama. She was always so quiet and meek and laid back. I only saw her get frustrated and angry a couple of times, which was usually followed with shouting in Italian," Sarina explained with a laugh, "but then she would calm down and that would be the end of it. I always seem to be quick to temper, quick to frustration, quick to every emotion. Although I tend to be quiet at first, I always seem to run headfirst into a conversation, which sometimes gets me into trouble."

"That was your mother too, Sarina, but life changed her," Gigi explained. "But you also share the same quality of thinking before leaping into a big decision. You look at all your options and study each fairly. You have an eye for business, and I am finding that you have a great knowledge of running a vineyard, more than you think. Perhaps you were tutored by your mama in this and you didn't even realize it."

Sarina thought about her time with her mother. Memories of summers past rushed back. "Well, we did go visit wineries and vineyards every summer and she always insisted on tours and explanations and we would talk about what we learned the whole way home. She also had several magazine subscriptions about wineries and vineyards and the latest technologies and ideas regarding running them. It became our thing. We would pore over the magazines together and discuss each article. I feel kind of silly not making the connection until now. But that ended years ago, even before she got sick."

"She was preparing you for your future I suspect."

"Maybe?" Sarina frowned.

"You have the same lively, but giving and loving spirit your mother had, Sarina." Her great-grandmother continued. "It saddens me that you do not see it in yourself and that you feel lost."

Sarina glanced at Gigi. "I always felt lost growing up, like I was in the wrong place. And I have been trying to figure out who I am for a long time. Business and accounting made sense as it fell in my lap and I was good at it, but now I am not sure if that is what I am meant for."

"Business sense and accounting are two things needed in running a successful vineyard," Gigi tried to encourage.

Sarina smiled. "Perhaps." They sat in silence, studying each other.

Sarina cleared her throat. "I don't want to decide anything right now, but I am thinking about everything. I promise."

"Perhaps we should discuss again at harvest."

Sarina nodded. "That sounds good."

"Perfect."

Gigi stood and hugged Sarina. "Okay, I will let you finish and get to work. I will see you later."

"See you later," Sarina responded, watching her great-grandmother walk out of the room. Once the door was shut, she glanced at the clock and realized it was already after eight thirty. Sarina sprang into action. She took a couple more bites, grabbed her shoes and sweater, gathered the tray of breakfast items, and left the room. She rushed through the villa toward the kitchen. She had a meeting to get to.

At nine o'clock sharp Sarina stood outside the wine barn. She wore a maroon skirt with a white blouse that had tiny flowers of yellow and maroon sprinkled all over it. Over the blouse, she wore a pale-yellow sweater with sleeves that barely covered her elbows. She had pulled her hair back in a bun to appear more business-like and she wore a pair of black flats. She hoped she gave off the appearance of being professional.

Sarina checked the small watch she had around her wrist. It was now a few minutes past nine and she began to wonder if she had misunderstood Alfonso. She was trying to decide if she should go in search of her cousin when she heard footsteps behind her. She turned and saw Alfonso striding toward her, wearing his normal jeans and black T-shirt with two men flanking each side of him. Both men wore suits—one dark gray and one black. Both businessmen had their hair slicked back and both wore dark sunglasses. Sarina glanced at their fancy shoes and wondered if they were going to walk the entire grounds because they would never make it wearing those.

Alfonso stopped short of Sarina and made the introductions. "Gentlemen, this is my cousin Sarina. She will join us today. Sarina, this is Jarrod Fraser and Simon Steele."

Sarina held out her hand. "Hello, nice to meet both of you."

"Oh, you speak perfect English and without an Italian accent," Jarrod said.

"I grew up on a farm in Iowa so I suppose that would be why. I actually don't speak a lick of Italian."

The businessmen laughed while Alfonso smiled at Sarina. "Come, let's head into the barn," Alfonso said leading the way, and the tour began. Alfonso explained everything that was in the barn and the process they had from grapes, to harvest, and turning it into wine. He indicated a few times that there were a few family secrets that made the wine better, but that he wouldn't disclose that information.

The four walked out toward the vineyard next and as they strolled among the vines, Jarrod would stop occasionally, study the vines and grapes, and smile. Sarina could tell he knew what he was looking at. The tour ended several hours later, and they went to the wine tasting building, where the businessmen tasted several of the wines. They would smile, nod their heads, exchange looks, but neither spoke.

When they were done with the wine tasting, Jarrod pulled Sarina aside and said, "I couldn't help but notice, Sarina, that you didn't contribute much to the conversation."

Sarina explained, "I am here on holiday, visiting family. I help wherever I can. And today my cousin asked me to join the tour since I speak English so well."

She tried to listen in to the conversation Alfonso and Simon were having, but Jarrod kept distracting her with different questions. Sarina couldn't shake the uneasy feeling that grew as the conversations continued.

There is just something about this visit. Alfonso is keeping something from me. As though sensing Sarina's unease, Alfonso caught her eye and flashed a grin. She smiled back, feeling a little better, but something still seemed off.

Soon Alfonso and Simon joined Sarina and Jarrod, and the four walked out of the wine tasting room and toward the businessmen's waiting car. Jarrod walked beside Sarina and continued his conversation with her. Sarina tripped on a rock in the path and Jarrod steadied her.

Sarina smiled and thanked the man but tried to pull away from his grasp. He refused to let go and Sarina didn't want to be rude, so she allowed herself to be led along the path even though it made her uncomfortable. When they finally made it to where Simon and Jarrod's car was parked, Sarina let out a sigh of relief at being able to break free of Jarrod.

Simon and Alfonso continued with light conversation until Simon said, "This was a good visit and exactly what we were looking for, Alfonso. We appreciate your help." The two shook hands.

Simon nodded toward Sarina and said, "It was a pleasure, miss, perhaps we shall see each other again on our home soil." He turned and got into the rear seat.

Sarina noticed there was another person sitting in the front seat. She wasn't sure why but seeing that the businessmen had a driver annoyed her.

Jarrod interrupted Sarina's thoughts by grabbing her hand as though to shake it, but instead held it in between his own two hands. "Sarina, it was such a pleasure."

Surprising her, Jarrod lifted her hand up to his mouth and kissed it lightly. He flashed a smile Sarina was sure made most women melt. But it didn't have that effect on her. She didn't like this guy and she couldn't quite put her finger on why.

Sarina pulled her hand away. "It was nice meeting you, Mr. Fraser." She stepped back a few feet as though dismissing him.

But her actions only seemed to encourage Jarrod, and he stepped closer. "You know, Sarina, we will be in the country for a little while. Perhaps you and I can have dinner some evening."

Sarina recovered from the horror she was sure showed on her face and said, "Thank you, Mr. Fraser, for your kind offer, but I must refuse. I won't have the time."

"Well, perhaps I will be able to persuade you to change your mind."

"I doubt it but thank you just the same. Goodbye." Sarina turned and walked several feet away, dismissing the man completely. She turned back around just in time to see Jarrod nod at Alfonso and get into the car.

Once settled, Jarrod rolled his window down. "We will be in touch." He mumbled something to the driver, and they drove off.

A shiver ran up Sarina's spine and she started to walk away. She stopped when Alfonso said, "Well he was quite taken with you."

Sarina turned to her cousin. "Unwanted attention I assure you.

"You know it might have been good for business if you had said yes to his proposal," Alfonso said with a sneer.

Sarina's mouth dropped open, and she forced herself to recover enough to say, "Is that why you wanted me here?"

"Well," Alfonso explained. "Jarrod Fraser is known to be the lady's man and he loves a pretty face. I thought it might help."

Sarina glared at her cousin. "Don't use me as bait ever again, Alfonso. There is more to me than my face."

Alfonso laughed and walked away.

Sarina stomped off in the opposite direction. She was fuming at being used as a pawn when she happened upon Antonio walking toward her. Sarina was still reeling so she almost missed the strange expression Antonio had on his face.

"Who was that?" Antonio asked while blocking Sarina from walking past him.

"What's it to you?" Sarina snapped.

"You could have told me you had a boyfriend," Antonio huffed.

"Oh, for the love of—he isn't my boyfriend." Sarina raised her voice. "I was helping Alfonso give a tour to some businessmen today, okay."

"Really, well they looked like greasy con men to me."

They did to Sarina too, but she wouldn't give Antonio the satisfaction. "Well, they seemed like perfect gentlemen to me. In fact, one of them asked me on a date."

"The one you were holding hands with no less."

"Really, Antonio, I don't see why you would care one bit."

"You don't, huh." Throwing up his hands in frustration, Antonio muttered something in Italian and walked away.

Sarina watched him go, puzzled by the whole encounter. Antonio continued to mutter in Italian with his arms flying about as though he were berating himself. Or was he berating her? She couldn't tell. She didn't think he even saw Sofia who had to dodge Antonio as he walked past. Sarina heard Sofia try to say something, but he kept walking.

Sarina sat on a bench, seething after the day's events with the businessmen and the encounter she had with Antonio. She fidgeted in her seat while she thought about everything. She felt bad for getting upset with Antonio and tried to figure out why she was more bothered by his behavior than the businessmen. She didn't understand why her heart and pride felt bruised by it. Someone sat next to her, and Sarina jumped. "Oh."

"Eh, I'm sorry, cousin. I didn't mean to startle you," Sofia said.

Sarina let out a slow breath and looked at Sofia wide eyed. "It's okay. It's just been a very strange day."

"Hmmm."

Sarina sat listening to the sound of the villa's daily activities. She stared at the vineyard, but she could feel Sofia studying her.

Sofia broke the silence. "Perhaps it isn't my place to say anything, but I have to tell you that Antonio appears to like you. I mean really like you."

"What?" Sarina turned to look at Sofia. "You could have fooled me."

"The actions of a jealous lover are usually confusing."

"We are not lovers, Sofia."

"Perhaps not, but there is something there between you two. I can see it."

"I think you are seeing things. There hasn't been more than a few words passed between us."

"Well, I know jealousy when I see it and Antonio was raging with it."

Sarina half smiled. "Really?"

"Yes." Sofia laughed then changed the subject. "Who were those men?"

"You didn't know?"

"No, but Alfonso doesn't share much of what he does for the vineyard with me," Sofia said.

Sarina frowned. "I would think he would, considering this is a family business and all."

"It is a family business but sometimes I get the impression that Alfonso looks at it as his business."

Sarina felt the unease from earlier return, and she realized it was time to discuss the questions she had about the ledger with her great-uncle. And she needed to do it sooner rather than later. But for now, she was going to enjoy the few minutes of time with Sofia.

The conversation changed to the weather, the vineyard, and Sofia shared about her friend Leone. "His family moved to the area several years ago and the first time I met him I was so put off by him that it took him a couple tries before I said yes to going out with him."

"Really?" Sarina asked. "I never would have guessed. The way you talk about him now seems like you really do care for him.

"I do. Now. But it took a little bit." Sofia tried to explain, "I guess I was afraid of falling for someone and I thought for sure I wouldn't stay here. But time changed that."

"I'm surprised you ever wanted to leave here," Sarina said.

"I know you are struggling with what to do, Sarina, so if I could give you some advice. Give it time. Don't rush things. And really look and be open to what this place has for you. Or could have for you. And of course, remember we are your family. Even if we were all strangers only a short time ago."

Sarina nodded. "Thank you for that. And I am giving it time."

"Good."

Sarina and Sofia stood and walked toward the villa. They decided to eat lunch together and Sofia offered to have Sarina shadow her for the day. Sarina really enjoyed the friendship that was developing between her and Sofia. As they started to walk into the villa, Sofia gave Sarina a quick hug. "I am glad you are here, cousin."

"Me too," Sarina said and followed her cousin inside.

Chapter Eleven

Sarina was elbows deep in grapevines learning about the different types of grapes they grew when Sofia hollered for her from the end of the row. She'd been working in the vineyard for several hours and was thankful for a break. "I don't see how I'm going to remember all of this," Sarina said as she walked toward Sofia.

"You will remember it all eventually. I promise," Sofia said. "How about you take a break from what you are doing and help me with taking a wine and goat cheese order into town."

"Oh, I would love that," Sarina said. She turned, hollered to Lorenzo she was leaving, and followed Sofia out of the vineyard. Going into town with Sofia would be fun, but it would also be a nice distraction. It had been a difficult morning working so closely with Antonio. They had not spoken much since their last encounter, and it was becoming more uncomfortable for her. She tried to reason that it was because of their disagreement, but Sarina knew it was more than that. She was increasingly more aware of when Antonio was near, and her heart would pound if he looked her way. Little sparks would zing through her if his hand brushed hers.

She sauntered past where Antonio was working, and the expression that passed between them made her cheeks warm. Her pulse quickened and she wondered if Antonio was feeling the same. *None of this matters, unless I make up with him. It doesn't matter if he was acting jealous, I shouldn't have yelled at him or tried to make him feel worse.* Sarina turned her head to catch one last glimpse of Antonio and caught him watching her. Sarina felt her face soften and she instinctively waved.

Antonio flashed a devilish grin and waved in return.

Perhaps things will be okay between us after all.

When Sarina and Sofia made it back to the villa, Sarina quickly cleaned up and met Sofia outside where her cousin was waiting in a pick-up truck. She noticed it had the vineyards logo on the side and found it gave her a sense of pride. Sarina climbed into the front seat next to Sofia and smiled at her. "It's such a beautiful day isn't it?"

Sofia nodded. "Are you ready then?"

"Yes, sorry to keep you waiting."

Sofia waved her hand in the air as if dismissing Sarina's apology. "You are fine. I am glad you are coming with me. This is a good lesson for you on a different aspect of the business, but it also gives us time to gossip about things going on."

Sarina laughed while Sofia put the vehicle into drive and drove toward town. The two cousins talked about the weather, the view of the countryside, the beauty of the town nestled by the sea, until Sofia abruptly changed the subject. "I think I am in love, Sarina, and I don't know what to do about it!"

Sarina swung her head toward Sofia. "Why do you need to do anything about it?"

"Well, he isn't exactly from the wealthiest of families and he isn't originally from here. I am not sure what would happen if this became more serious. I don't want to leave the family business, but he is intent on working his own family business. I just don't know what to do."

"I would think you should follow your heart and what is meant to be, will be."

"Maybe."

"Has he mentioned how he feels to you?" Sarina asked.

"No, he hasn't which worries me." Sofia frowned. "There are a few women in the village who have their eye on him, and I can't help but be a little jealous, and a little fearful that he doesn't feel the same about me."

"Have you thought about talking to him about it?" Sarina asked. "Find out where you're at in your commitment to each other and the relationship?"

"I couldn't bring it up first," Sofia cried. "I would think he should do that."

"Oh, come on, Sofia," Sarina scoffed. "It's not the stone age."

Sofia smirked. "You are right, Sarina"—pausing as though contemplating something—"I will talk to him about it. Thank you for your advice."

"You're welcome, but if it backfires, you got this advice from someone else, okay?"

Sofia giggled and said, "Oh, Sarina, I love you, dear cousin."

Sarina joined in her cousin's laughter. "I love you too." Sarina sobered. "What do you think the family will say about him?"

"Oh no. The famiglia." Sofia's expression grew anxious. "They will most likely scare him away."

"What? Hasn't he been to the villa or to Nonna's house?" Sarina asked. "Or your parents' house for that matter?"

Sofia shrugged. "No, I have been holding off on doing that."

"I can understand why. You should just rip the band aid off and invite him to the next family dinner."

"Rip the band aid off?" Sofia asked.

"Never mind," Sarina said. "But seriously, you should invite him over this Sunday."

"Oy, that makes me sweat thinking about it."

Sofia and Sarina broke into laughter at the same time. They were still laughing when Sofia stopped at the rear of her brothers' restaurant. Sofia honked the horn, got out of the truck, walked to the back, and lowered the tailgate. Sarina followed suit and the two unloaded a case of wine.

Tito came out the rear door, called a greeting to them, and assisted with unloading. Tito told Sofia and Sarina to find a place to sit, and he would make something for them to eat.

"You know, Sarina," Sofia said as she sat at the bar. "He never offers to make me something to eat when it is just me making the delivery."

"That's a lie," Tito called from the kitchen. Sarina and Sofia chuckled.

Sarina joined the banter by saying something witty, which made Sofia laugh harder. Sarina started to say something else when an older man at the end of the bar turned toward her. She quieted and frowned when he didn't stop staring at her.

The man appeared to be visibly shaken. He spilled the liquid in his glass down his hand and onto the bar. Sarina tried to smile at the man, but this seemed to upset him even more. He called to a young woman who was working behind the bar, said something in Italian, and turned back to continue staring at Sarina. The longer he stared, the more agitated he became.

Sarina heard Sofia ramble in Italian, and she turned to see her cousin looking at the man. She glanced back at the man just as he tore his eyes away from her, answered Sofia, and turned his gaze back on Sarina.

Sarina shifted in her seat and asked Sofia, "Should I know that guy?"

The man's face paled and he started to rush the young woman who was helping him. He was so agitated he was all but yelling. Tito came out from the kitchen, went to stand next to the man, and asked, "What seems to be the trouble here, Marco?"

The man called Marco glanced at Tito and back to Sarina, gesturing wildly toward her.

As though it dawned on Tito what the issue might be, he said, "You have not met my cousin Sarina yet. But I am sure you knew she was here."

The man nodded, grabbed his change, backed away from the bar, and all but ran out of the restaurant.

Sarina looked from Sofia to Tito and asked, "Who was that?"

Tito frowned. "That was Marco. He grew up the same time as your mother."

"I am so confused," Sarina said. "Why would he act that way?"

Sofia and Tito exchanged glances. Sofia cleared her throat. "I am sure it is nothing."

Sarina didn't miss the exchange between brother and sister, and she felt her confusion turn to frustration. *This must all be related to Mama's secret.* She stood, stepped back from the bar, and asked Sofia, "Will you please tell me who that man was?

Sofia shook her head. "I'm sorry, Sarina."

Sarina had enough. "For the love of—why is it that no one will tell me anything?" Her hands began to shake, and she tried to stay calm but instead shouted, "Everyone has this secret about *my* mother, and no one is willing to tell me about it! I am so tired of this!"

Alessandro came rushing from the kitchen, and Sarina assumed he must have heard her outburst. Sarina sat back down on the stool, realizing that other people in the restaurant were muttering things in Italian. Sarina knew they were talking about her or at least her mother because they kept saying Luciana.

Sarina buried her face in her hands and moaned. She felt arms wrap around her and Sofia said, "I'm sorry, Sarina."

"Come, let's go to the back," Alessandro said.

I shouldn't have blown up at them. But I am so tired of secrets. Sarina slid off her stool and stumbled.

Alessandro grabbed her arm. "I got you."

Tears were running down Sarina's cheeks by the time they made it safely to the back. She looked over and noticed Sofia's eyes were wet with tears as well.

Alessandro took a deep breath. "Sarina, I can't imagine how difficult this must be for you, but we had to swear that we would not say anything."

"Say anything about what?" Sarina choked out.

Sofia put her arm around Sarina. "I will talk to Nonna and beg her to talk with you. It is only fair and right that you know. But please understand it is difficult for her to talk about it. And we have only been trying to protect you."

Sarina studied Sofia and realized how she must have come across. Her eyes grew wide. "Oh my—Sofia—I was so rude to you. I am so sorry."

Sofia waved her hand in the air as though to dismiss Sarina's apology. "If you can't yell at family, who can you yell at?"

Sarina smiled. Sofia pressed her forehead against Sarina's. "Are you sure you want to know, Sarina? Perhaps your mother didn't want you to know for fear that it would change how you looked at her. And the last thing she would want is for you to view her as something different than how you saw her."

Sarina pulled away from Sofia. "How awful is it?"

"That will be for you to decide, Sarina," Tito said.

Sarina felt sick to her stomach and asked to go back to the vineyard.

Sofia nodded, exchanged looks with her brothers, and she and Sarina left. They rode in silence to the vineyard while Sarina stared out the window. When they finally pulled into the villa driveway and parked, Sofia reached over, squeezed Sarina's hand. Sarina smiled at her, climbed out of the truck, and went inside.

Sarina stomped past anyone she saw without a word and went up to her room. She shoved at her door, which didn't latch, and flung herself on the bed. She sobbed into her pillow until she heard Gigi and Sofia talking in the hallway.

"What happened?" Gigi asked.

"Marco was at the restaurant and he acted as though he had seen a ghost," Sofia explained. "Sarina could tell by the reaction of everyone, that it had to do with Aunt Luc, and she became terribly upset. Someone needs talk to her. We can't keep it from her any longer."

"Yes, I will call, Giada."

Sarina heard footsteps retreat so she got up from her bed to shut her door. She paused when she heard Gigi talking to someone on her phone.

"It's time. We have to tell her."

Chapter Twelve

Sarina glanced around the room while her eyes adjusted to the light. She could tell by the way the sun was shining through the opened door of her balcony that it was the middle of the afternoon. She sat up and rubbed her swollen eyes but jumped when she saw her grandmother sitting on the edge of the bed.

Nonna smiled sadly at Sarina, turned her head, and looked out the window.

Sarina was about to say something when her grandmother started talking as though she were in a trance.

"Your mother," Nonna started, stopped, took a deep breath. "Your mother was so full of life. So vibrant and happy. She knew what she wanted, and who she wanted to spend her life with from the time she was fourteen. She spent most of her time with your great-grandmother and the villa, and when she was home all she could talk about was the vineyard.

"As I am sure you have guessed by now, she almost married Stefano. She was barely nineteen, but she was so happy." Sarina's grandmother laughed. "The two were head over heels in love, but they also fought

like cats and dogs. There was such fiery passion between them. So, I guess that would mean there would
be fighting. The electric bond that brought them together was so vibrant."

Her grandmother paused as though she were
catching her breath. "It was the night of the festival.
Your mother and Stefano had been fighting all day."

"Over what?" Sarina asked.

"You know it was so long ago, I don't remember,"
Nonna explained. "In fact, they probably wouldn't remember either. Luc, your mother, had stormed off
from Stefano at some point in the evening and she
said she was going to head home to the vineyard instead of staying in town. Exasperated, Stefano let her
go and tried to join in the fun, but Valentina, your
mother's closest friend, encouraged Stefano to go after her."

She stopped again and appeared to be struggling
with how to continue. She sighed. "We are not sure
what happened from the time your mother left
Stefano and the time he caught up with her. But when
he found her, Luc was sobbing, her dress was torn,
and she was covered in blood. She was holding a knife
and standing over Bernado Bianchi's dead body."

Sarina gasped and her hands began to tremble.
Tears rained down and she realized they matched the

tears on her grandmother's face. Sarina took a deep breath. "What—what happened?"

Her grandmother turned to her. "No one knows. Your mother couldn't remember because she had a head injury. She had a gash on the back of her head, and scratches, blood and bruises all over her body. She told Stefano that she noticed the knife and picked it up before he had come around the corner. She told the police the same."

Sarina reached out her trembling hand to rest it on her grandmother's hand. Nonna looked over at her and Sarina flinched at the pain in the woman's eyes.

Nonna patted the top of Sarina's hand and continued. "Since there were no witnesses and really no evidence to explain what happened, the police seemed to think that your mother came upon Bernado either being attacked and was attacked herself, or they were walking together, and someone attacked them. But it is really a mystery that no one seemed able to solve."

Her grandmother stood, walked over to the window, and looked out. "Stefano blamed himself because he let your mother leave by herself. But she blamed herself, and until the day of her death she believed she had done something terrible." She looked back at Sarina. "She was no doubt attacked and she had nightmares for weeks after. They were so awful at times, she couldn't be consoled. Stefano grew increasingly frustrated with her because she began to pull away from him. She said she couldn't remember what happened, but by this time the town was talking and thought perhaps she killed Bernado."

Sarina walked over to stand next to her grandmother.

"A few days before the harvest that following year," her grandmother continued, "your mama broke things off with Stefano, saying she was too broken for him, that he needed to go on with life with someone who was whole. She told us she wanted to go to my sister's in Germany and eventually go to school there where my sister's husband taught. She had already been in correspondence with them and they had agreed to have her stay with them as long as it was okay with me and her father, your grandfather."

Sarina studied her grandmother. "Did you try to stop her?"

"What was I to say? She seemed so shattered and scared and lost. And it was the first thing she was really excited about in so long. So, we let her go."

"Did she really think she killed Bernado?" Sarina whispered.

"Yes, I think she did. Or at least felt partly to blame, especially because of the way she left the festivities and Stefano that night."

he looked toward the house. He started to walk in the direction of his gaze when Sofia reached out and stopped him. Whatever Sofia said to stop his advance seemed to resonate with him because Antonio stopped, looked back up toward the house, turned, and stomped back to the vineyard.

The sun started to lower in the sky so Nonna stood, walked over to Sarina, and cupped her face in her hand. "I'm so sorry you had to hear these tragic things, but it was time you knew, as the town will continue to talk the longer you are here."

Sarina nodded. "Thank you for sharing this with me. I know it must have been difficult to do so."

"It is not something I like to think on or talk about often."

Sarina realized she would not be able to discuss this with Nonna again. She watched her grandmother leave and a few minutes later she caught a glimpse of her elder climbing into her car and she was gone.

"This was not easy for her," Gigi broke the silence. "It has been difficult for her all these years, losing Luc. Yes, she didn't pass away until recently but, in some ways, she lost her long ago. And Giada has struggled with it. A mother's love for her children is something no one understands unless they experience it."

"I can't help but wonder if there is some way to figure out what happened," Sarina said staring out at the vineyard.

"That is the very question many have asked. But no one has had the courage to dig for answers. Most believe the past is best left in the past."

Sarina decided she would not rest until she found out more, even if it hurt her and the family. She prayed for strength and courage while she went down this path. A storm was coming, and opening old wounds in this community was not going to be easy for any of them, but she believed she had to find out the truth so that her mother could truly rest in peace.

"Perhaps it is time," Gigi said as though she read Sarina's thoughts. "And perhaps you, Sarina, are just the one to put this whole thing to rest once and for all."

Chapter Thirteen

Sarina studied the ledger in front of her and noticed the same tick mark that continued to cause her concern. Every time it appeared something was missing, or an account of the funds was incorrect. She wondered if there was another ledger Alfonso or even her great-uncle had that she could study so things would balance in those places.

Sarina realized she couldn't put off discussing this with her great-uncle any longer. So, she went to go find him. When she knocked on his bedroom door there was no answer. Sarina peeked inside and found the room empty.

Something in the back of her mind told her she was running out of time and it was time to ask some difficult questions.

As she made her way downstairs to look for him outside, she saw Sofia coming in. They locked eyes and Sofia rushed toward Sarina, pulling her into a long hug. Sofia pulled away slightly and looked at her quizzically. "How are you holding up?"

Sarina smiled. "I am actually okay. It is a bit of a relief to finally know but I still feel like there is more that I need to find out."

"I think we all felt that way once we heard the story for the first time. But no one pursues it."

"Maybe it's time."

Sofia's smile widened. "Perhaps you are right. Let me know if I can help."

"I will." They talked of other things and walked together into the kitchen. Sarina heard her stomach growl and realized it was lunch time.

"Ha, I am hungry too," Sofia said, and the two laughed.

Sarina hadn't forgotten about her mission to find her great-uncle but decided to eat first.

Sarina and Sofia took their lunch out back and were eating in the flower garden when Antonio happened upon them. He smiled and said, "Hello," but Sarina couldn't help notice the concern in his eyes as he studied her.

"Hello. And I'm fine," Sarina said.

"I'm happy to hear it. But if you need anything, please let me know. I am here for you," Antonio said, his cheeks turning red. "That is to say I—well ..."

Sarina laughed. "Antonio, you are so cute when you're flustered."

This seemed to do the trick, for the light returned to Antonio's eyes and his mischievous grin came back. "You think I'm cute?"

Sarina tilted her head. "Maybe."

"You tease me."

"Perhaps."

Antonio laughed. "Will you not allow me to take you out for dinner? We can even go to your cousins' restaurant if it would make you feel more comfortable."

Sarina studied him. She hoped she hid the war raging inside of her. She was really drawn to him. But her mother's past with this man's father put a wrench in things. "I need to think about it, Antonio."

"Isn't that what you were doing when you were keeping me on the edge of my seat by your silence?"

"Yes." Sarina frowned. "With our family's history though ..." she let her words trail off.

Antonio nodded. "I thought of that, but I can't seem to stay away from you, Sarina."

The change in Antonio's tone did not escape her, and she knew her response could cause a shift in their ... relationship ... in whatever way she chose to define what was going on between them.

Sarina looked past Antonio. When he acted like he was about to give up, she said, "Perhaps we could take a couple of walks first, get to know one another a little more. Then if we think this might work—well let's see how things go."

Antonio smiled, bowed in front of Sarina, took her hand gingerly, and skimmed one finger across it. "I will be by after dinner this evening. You and I can walk among the vineyard, just the two of us and ... talk."

Sarina sucked in her breath. "See you then."

Antonio leaned in closer. Her heart pounded so loud she thought for sure he could hear it. He pulled back, let go of Sarina's hand. "Until tonight."

Sarina stared after him until he was at the edge of the vineyard where he stopped, turned, waved, and walked out of sight.

Sofia cleared her throat. Sarina jumped and slammed her hand against her chest. "Oh, for the love of—Sofia, why didn't you say something or give me a hint that you were still sitting here?"

Sofia howled and said, "Because I was too busy enjoying the show."

"Ha—Ha." Sarina rolled her eyes. She contemplated things with Antonio and asked, "Do you think this is a mistake ... well ... considering everything?"

"No, Sarina, I don't. I think it's fantastic," Sofia said. "And who knows, maybe this is what fate had in mind all along."

"Maybe," Sarina mumbled.

Sofia appeared to be pleased with Sarina's encounter with Antonio, but Sarina worried that maybe it wasn't a good idea. *But he sure is cute. Maybe Sofia is right. Maybe this is how things were meant to be after all.*

Later that evening, Antonio arrived earlier than what Sarina had planned, and she was still eating with the family in the courtyard. Sofia winked at her across the table, and Sarina realized Sofia noticed Antonio at the same time she did. As Antonio walked toward the group, Gigi called a greeting and told him to grab a plate from the kitchen and eat with them. He smiled and disappeared into the kitchen, emerging a few minutes later with a plate and another basket of bread.

He set the bread on the table and sat next to Sofia. Sarina was sitting across the table from him and she felt the blood rushing into her face when he smiled at her. She prayed she wasn't as red as she thought she was, but looking at Sofia trying not to laugh confirmed she was indeed that red.

Alfonso cleared his throat and Sarina glanced his way. He hadn't said much throughout dinner but was polite when Antonio showed up. Sarina still felt that something was off with how Alfonso was handling the books. She hadn't spoken to her great-uncle about what she found yet, and she felt she couldn't say anything to anyone else about it.

Sarina's grandfather asked Antonio how his parents were, pulling Sarina from her thoughts, back to

Antonio's visit. They conversed about his family and what they were doing that evening. Sarina felt her grandmother's eyes on her but when she looked over at Nonna, she had a guarded look. She glanced at Gigi, who had a pleased expression on her face, so Sarina tried not to worry about how they would feel about her and Antonio spending time together.

As dinner began to wind down and the family started to scatter to other chairs or other activities, Sarina and Antonio took their leave and walked toward the vineyard. They had reached the other side of the garden when Antonio reached out and grasped Sarina's hand in his.

Sarina enjoyed the feeling of their hands entwined, while Antonio pointed out different aspects of the vineyard and his work. Not wanting to affect his enthusiasm, Sarina gently asked what he wanted to do with his knowledge in the future.

Antonio paused as though he were collecting his thoughts and said, "Run my own vineyard and winery. I love the feel of the dirt on my fingers and watching the grapes grow into little beauties. Then the harvest of the grapes is like a romantic song that has finally reached its climax. The taste of the wine on your tongue the first time is a wonderful burst of accomplishment knowing you brought this wine to life."

Sarina beamed watching Antonio talk, and she wondered if he had plans of finding some place local. She didn't like the thought of him not being at the villa. *I'm getting ahead of myself.* They were not exactly dating, yet she couldn't imagine spending time with any other man. But she had not decided if she was going to stay in Italy or go home to Iowa, so having thoughts of a future with Antonio was a bit premature. And yet, her mind wouldn't stop spinning in that direction.

Thinking of Iowa made her frown and Antonio stopped walking. "What's wrong? Are you okay? Did I say something?"

Sarina shook her head. "No, I was listening to you talk and I thought of my home in Neely."

Antonio nodded. "Are you hoping to return some day?"

"I don't know what I am going to do," she tried to explain. "Right now, I am taking it a day at a time. I imagine I will have to return at some point to get my affairs in order there, even if I decide to stay here."

"Do you have a lot to take care of?" he asked.

"There is the farm. And a job if I choose to go back to it," Sarina said.

"No family or friends?" Antonio asked.

"I have people who care about me," Sarina said, "neighbors and such, but no close friends and my American family is no longer living."

"What is pulling you back there?"

Sarina looked off in the distance and thought about what it could be. "I believe it is my loyalty to my father and the farm that was left in my keeping."

"Devotion to family and all they hold dear." Antonio smiled. "That is such a Giacoletti family trait. This does not surprise me really. You are as much a Giacoletti as any of them."

Sarina smiled. "Thank you. In some ways I feel more at home here than I ever did back in Iowa but—"

"But you feel like you are betraying your father by jumping headfirst into committing to the Giacoletti Vineyard and Winery," Antonio finished for her.

"Yes, that is exactly what I am feeling," Sarina said. "I couldn't quite put my finger on it until now. I feel so torn."

"That is a normal way to feel for one who loves her family, all of them, so deeply," Antonio said. "My heart hurts for you and I do not envy your situation. Please know I am here for you and will try to help any way I can."

"Okay, tell me what I should do," Sarina said with a laugh.

Antonio laughed. "That is not something I can do. I would love for you to stay. But this is a decision that you alone have to make."

"I know," Sarina said, her shoulders slumped forward. "I'm so afraid I'm going to make the wrong decision."

"Perhaps you should look at all the reasons why you should stay, then look at all the reasons why you should go," Antonio offered. "If the stay column wins over the go column then maybe that is what you should do."

"I wish it were that simple," Sarina said. "I just—well I just don't know if it could be that simple."

"Maybe it is."

"It seems like such a monumental decision though," Sarina said. "I feel like it should be something significant telling me to stay or go."

"Perhaps, but maybe it truly is as simple as knowing where you belong and where you feel most at home," Antonio said.

Sarina nodded. "Perhaps we should change the subject. I didn't want this to be so serious."

"When we are together, Sarina, you can talk to me about anything even if it is serious," he said.

Sarina smiled at him and they started walking again.

The rest of the evening they talked about their childhoods. Antonio shared what it was like growing up and going to school with the Giacoletti family. He explained that he spent many hours running through the vineyard during the summer and counted the days during the school year for when he could return to the vineyard.

Sarina shared stories of her life on the farm and the fun times she had with her parents. And what it was like trying to make her mother happy after her father died. They laughed so hard at times they almost cried and cried when talking about loved ones gone.

As they began walking back toward the villa Antonio asked, "Was it hard for you, Sarina?"

Sarina flinched, stopped walking, and turned toward him.

Antonio lifted his hand and brushed a stray strand of hair behind her ear. "Was it hard for you with your mother I mean?"

Sarina knew what he'd meant; she just wasn't expecting the question. And although his gentleness was unexpected, it touched her. "Yes, yes it was. There were days when the pain was so intense all Mama could do was lay there and cry. I felt so helpless. When it was nearing the end, I used to pray that her suffering would finally end, but then I would feel horrible about that because she was my mother and I loved her." Sarina paused, placing her hand over the ache in her chest. "And now, I miss her every day."

"I can only imagine what it must have been like for you. I wish I knew you then so that I could have helped or been a comfort to you."

Sarina smiled and kissed him on the cheek. His eyes grew wide, flamed with desire, and he pulled her to him. The kiss started with a hint of desperation, but it moved into a gentleness that rippled through Sarina and she melted further into his embrace. When they pulled apart, they studied one another until Antonio broke the silence. "I think you should put that down on your 'I should stay' list."

Sarina laughed and hugged him. They held each other close as he kissed the top of her head and she sighed. "Do you think your father would talk to me about my mother and ... and ... well ..."

"About what happened," Antonio finished for her.

She pulled away from him enough to study his face. "Yes, to talk about what happened."

"He might. You should go see him," Antonio said. "My mother and father will be home tomorrow since it is Saturday. You could have Sofia drive you and drop you off tomorrow morning. I have work to do here tomorrow afternoon so I can bring you back myself after you visit."

"That would be wonderful," Sarina said, but her eyes grew wide when she thought how this might be uncomfortable for Antonio and his mother.

"I am so sorry I didn't even think that this might be an awkward situation for you and your mom," Sarina said as she attempted to read Antonio's expression.

Antonio pulled away from Sarina, smiled down at her. He grabbed her hand and they started walking again. "No need to worry for us, Sarina," Antonio said. "Your mother and my father may have been lovers at one point in their history but there is a love between my parents that they didn't have. Your mother and my father had a young love. An immature love in a lot of ways. And my parents have a love and respect for one another that has built their marriage into a lasting one. I never doubt their love for one another. And besides all that, you must remember that my mother and your mother were best friends growing up."

"Oh yeah, I forgot about that," Sarina said.

"They were extremely close," Antonio said.

"Okay," Sarina considered everything he'd shared, cleared her throat, and said, "I will figure out the details with Sofia and head over after breakfast in the morning."

"I will let them know you are coming then," Antonio said with a smile.

They walked the rest of the way in silence and as they neared the house, the sun was beginning to set. Sarina could hear her grandparents and Gigi talking as they stood. Her grandparents appeared to be preparing to leave. She started to rush over to say her goodbyes but halted when she heard her name mentioned. Sarina stood in the shadows, her heart pounding, while she listened to her elders talk about her and Antonio.

"I don't like it," Nonna said.

"I know this brings up old memories," Gigi said.

"Well, we best not interfere and who knows it may be a good thing," Sarina's grandfather interjected while he patted Nonna's arm. "It will be alright, my love."

"I agree with Cosimo," Gigi said. "I have a feeling it will be good."

"I just don't want her hurt," Nonna said. "She has suffered enough already."

"Haven't we all, dear," Sarina's grandfather said.

"Yes but ..."

"She isn't Luc, Giada," Sarina's grandfather interrupted. "She is her own person and even though she has Luc's spark she has a level head on her shoulders and knows her own mind. She has already seen enough of life to know to be cautious."

"Perhaps you are right, Cosimo. I just ..." Nonna trailed off.

"We all feel responsible for her," Gigi added. "But we don't want to push her away either. She is an adult after all and still has ties to America, enough that if we push too hard, she may leave us."

Sarina's elders turned their conversation to the weather and she waited another moment before walking over to them. She didn't want them to know she had heard them, and she wasn't sure how she felt about what they had said. She could feel Antonio studying her, but she forced a smile and walked into the circle of light surrounding the campfire where she said her goodbyes to Nonna and her grandfather.

Sarina watched her grandparents leave and as she walked toward a seat by the fire, she heard Gigi ask, "Would you care for a glass of wine, Antonio?"

Sarina saw Antonio glance her way before responding. "Actually no, I need to get home. I need to prepare for a visitor tomorrow."

Sarina felt the heat in her cheeks.

"Okay." Gigi paused and appeared to study Sarina and Antonio for a moment before asking, "Will we see you tomorrow?"

"Yes," Antonio said. "I actually have a few things I need to get done."

"It is as I expected," Gigi said. "Why don't you stay for dinner tomorrow and invite your parents to come out too."

"They would enjoy that, thank you."

Antonio said his goodbyes to everyone but paused in front of Sarina. "I had a wonderful evening. See you tomorrow." Antonio kissed Sarina on the cheek and walked to his car whistling a tune. When he got to his car, he started to get in but paused. He looked over at Sarina, who was watching him, flashed a cocky grin, waved, and climbed into his car.

As his car drove out of sight Sofia went to stand next to Sarina and said, "Okay, tell us all about it."

Sarina giggled, looked over at Gigi who winked at her, and said, "It was lovely."

"Lovely?" Sofia asked. "That's all we get?"

"Yes, it is," Sarina said with a laugh. "Oh, and by the way, I need a ride to Antonio's house in the morning."

Sarina walked toward the house. Sofia followed close behind, trying to get more information out of her but failed.

Chapter Fourteen

Sofia dropped Sarina in front of a large stone home on the outskirts of town. It sat on the edge of a bluff which overlooked the sea. It appeared to be much like her grandparents' with a small garden in front. It had modern updates on the outside, even though it appeared to have been built hundreds of years ago. Sarina knocked on the door and didn't have to wait long for an older woman to answer.

"Sarina," she said. "It is wonderful to finally meet you at last." She pulled Sarina into a hug, and Sarina was sure her eyes were wide when they pulled apart. "Forgive me, I am Valentina," the older woman explained. "I was so close to your mother when we were growing up."

Sarina recognized her as the woman in the street with Antonio the day Sarina met him. "Hello, it is wonderful to meet you."

"Please come in, Sarina," Valentia said. "Would you like a coffee, perhaps, or something else to drink?"

"Coffee would be lovely. Thank you," Sarina said as she followed Valentina.

Stefano walked into the front room as Sarina cleared the doorway.

"Hello," Stefano said pulling Sarina into an exuberant hug.

Sarina saw Antonio over Stefano's shoulder and he winked at her. Antonio looked pleased with how things were going so far.

Sarina wasn't sure how she should greet Antonio after their "date" the night before, but Antonio handled that for her. He pulled her into a hug, kissed her on the cheek, and as he pulled away, he snagged her hand and said, "I trust you slept well, mi amore."

"Yes," Sarina said, smiling up at Antonio. "And you?"

"Alas, I could only think of you, so sleep did not come so quickly," he whispered.

Stefano cleared his throat. "We are heading out into the garden if you want to join us there."

Heat flamed Sarina's cheeks as she followed Antonio through the house and outside. The garden was much the same vegetation and flowers as her grandparents', but it had a unique layout and the view of the sea, although different, was just as breathtaking.

Sarina commented on the lovely home and garden, and Valentina thanked her. Valentina poured coffee and the four sat around a bistro style table.

Valentina seemed to be studying Antonio and her closely. Sarina wondered how much Antonio had shared with his parents, and how much their actions gave away their feelings for each other. Valentina looked concerned and Sarina wondered what she must be thinking about the situation and if it had anything to do with Sarina's lack of commitment to staying in Italy.

Valentina confirmed Sarina's thoughts by asking, "So Sarina, how long do you plan to stay in Italy?"

"That remains to be seen. I have been given an offer to stay permanently but—"

"But she is loyal to both sides of her family," Antonio said jumping in and giving his mother a look as if to say, stop it, I know what you are doing.

Valentina smiled at him, turned to Sarina, and said, "Well I hope we can persuade you to stay."

"I am looking at all my options," Sarina said.

"It's not an easy thing sometimes when deciding your future," Stefano interjected.

"No, it's not," Sarina said.

"Well, I pray you find your answer soon," Valentina said.

"Thank you," Sarina said.

Valentina stood. "I almost forgot, Sarina, can you come with me? I would like to show you something."

Puzzled, Sarina followed Valentina into the house and upstairs to a bedroom. Sarina paused inside the door as Valentina pulled a small box from underneath the bed. After placing it on the bed, Valentina said, "Come."

Sarina crossed the room and stood next to her as she opened the box. It held old pictures and various other objects that one would store in a keepsake box.

Valentina brushed at her cheek as though wiping a tear away and Sarina wondered at the emotion. "I have to tell you, Sarina, seeing you has brought back so many memories. Your mother was my best friend. We were more like sisters and I miss her."

Sarina nodded. "Were you able to keep in touch after she left?"

"Yes. We wrote each other often after she moved to Germany. But when she moved to America our letters were not as frequent, but they didn't have to be. We wrote when we could and once a year we talked on the phone. Well, until the last couple of years anyway. I think it just became too difficult for her to find the time to talk or write letters after your father died.

Sarina was surprised at how much her mother had kept in contact with her past, but had shared so little of it with her.

"You didn't know, did you?" Valentina asked.

"No, I didn't," Sarina said. "She kept so much from me I am finding."

"She was scared of her past and wanted to keep it from you as much as possible," Valentina said.

"Then why send me here now?" Sarina asked.

"Perhaps when one gets to the end of their life they reflect on things and try to rectify those things that perhaps they could have or should have done differently," Valentina said.

"Do you think my mother regretted not sharing this part of her life with me?" Sarina asked.

"I think your mother thought she would have more time to bring you here herself when she was ready," Valentina said. "But life had a different idea, and she didn't get the chance."

Sarina frowned and stared at the contents of the box. She noticed a picture of two young women sitting and laughing on the beach by the sea. One woman was a younger version of her mother and the other was a younger version of the woman standing next to Sarina.

Valentina lifted the picture Sarina had been staring at, studied it, and handed it to her. "We were so young here, barely out of school. We had decided to take a day off and spend it by the sea. The sea was one of your mother's favorite things. I often wondered how she managed to not have it near her living in Iowa all those years."

Sarina grinned, remembering her mother creating their own sea.

Valentina picked up another picture; it was one of Stefano and Sarina's mother standing arm in arm in front of an old pickup truck with the vineyard in the background. Valentina appeared wistful at what Sarina could only think was a distant memory. Valentina handed the picture to Sarina. "This picture was taken a week before—well a week ..." she trailed off.

"A week before ... it ... happened," Sarina finished.

Valentina studied Sarina. "That day changed all our lives. It rocked the village. People took sides, and your grandparents were desperate to make things right but didn't know how. It was a tough time."

"I'm sure me coming here has brought up things that some would prefer to stay buried," Sarina said while she studied the picture.

"Perhaps it is good that it is brought up again," Valentina said. "Perhaps it can be dealt with once and for all and the past can finally be buried and put to rest and peace can be once more where there is none."

"You are thinking of Bernado's father," Sarina said.

"Yes," Valentina agreed. "And your grandparents. And in some ways, my Stefano."

Sarina's eyes widened and she studied Valentina. "Does this bother you, me being here?"

"Oh no, dear child," Valentina said. "I am not a jealous woman. I only hurt for those that I love."

"What happened between you and my mother that you didn't stay as close?" Sarina asked.

"It—happened," Valentina said. "It changed her. She was so lost, so broken and she lived with a guilt she shouldn't have had, and she didn't know how to handle things or deal with it."

Valentina let out a sigh, took a deep breath, and continued, "The day she broke things off with Stefano she came to me crying and said that she loved him too much to continue to hurt him the way she was constantly doing in those days. She told me that she had to get away from here. I begged her not to go and to go back to Stefano, but she refused. She hugged me, said goodbye, and left. I didn't see your mother again until—well—until I went to Germany to ask her if it was okay for Stefano and me to be together."

"Wait. What?" Sarina said.

"Yes," Valentina explained. "Stefano and I were naturally drawn together by our grief at losing your mother the way we did."

Valentina shifted her feet and her shoulders slumped forward. "At first, we were just friends helping each other heal. But then the appreciation we had for one another grew into something more. I remember the day he kissed me the first time. I was thrilled, but I also felt like I was betraying your mother."

Valentina paused and stared at the picture Sarina still held in her hand. "It had been six months after she left when he kissed me, and I knew I had to go see her and talk with her. I explained to Stefano that this wouldn't work for us if I didn't have Luc's blessing."

"And she gave it whole-heartedly, didn't she?" Sarina asked.

"Yes, she did," Valentina said. "She had begun seeing your father by this point and said that what Stefano and she had was ... well ... what they had, died the same night as when ... it ... happened."

Valentina cleared her throat. "I asked your mother again if she could tell me what happened, but she still couldn't remember. She said it was all fuzzy like a bad dream she couldn't see clearly. When I saw her in Germany, she looked more at rest than I had seen her for a long time. I was glad of that and happy to see she was finding some peace."

Valentina picked up a couple more pictures and sifted through them. "When I returned to Italy and to Stefano things progressed quickly, and soon, we were engaged. We got married about a year after your mother left for Germany. I did ask your mother to come stand with me at the wedding, but she said she couldn't come back. Then three months later your mother came home for her wedding to your father before heading to America."

"Yes," Sarina said. "I heard that part. My parents came to Italy, the family met my dad, they got married, and they left for America, never to return."

"That's right," Valentina said, "While she was here, she never went into town and she only spoke with Stefano once, briefly. She told him she was sorry she had broken his heart but that it turned out better this way."

Valentina continued to sift through pictures. "When Stefano told me about it later, he explained that the shadows of that day were still there, but they were buried now, and we would probably never see her again."

"And he was right," Sarina said.

"Yes," Valentina said. "He was right. In some ways, her leaving helped him to bury his own shadows from that day. But I see them occasionally. I mentioned to you earlier I am not a jealous woman, but I am not a foolish one either. He will always love your mother, but he has a big heart and I know he loves me too. His love for me is different, it's solid but he still loves Luc and I think there is a part of him that won't ever rest because things were never fully resolved."

"My poor mother," Sarina whispered. "She had so many demons, and I never knew it. And I'm sorry for Stefano and for you."

"Ah, well, we as parents get really good at hiding our demons," Valentina said.

Sarina and Valentina continued to look through old pictures. They laughed or cried as Valentina shared stories with each picture until they reached a smaller box which rested at the bottom. Valentina lifted the box and opened it. Inside was an old scarf and two necklaces. The multicolored scarf was made of a soft silky material. The necklaces looked identical, only one was a blue flower and one was a yellow flower.

Valentina held the items, as though lost in thought. She turned to Sarina and said, "The scarf was your mother's. She let me borrow it the evening before she left for America, and when I tried to give it back to her, she told me to keep it until she returned."

Caressing the necklaces Valentina sighed, took a deep breath and said, "The necklaces were ones she bought for us when we were fifteen. It was my birthday present. She gave me the yellow one and she kept the blue one. Yellow was her favorite color and blue was my favorite color. She said that we should have each other's colors, that way when we looked at them, we would think of each other. It was a beautiful gift from a beautiful friend."

"How did you get both of them?" Sarina asked.

"She had been wearing her necklace the night of the incident," Valentina explained. "It had been broken at some point in the struggle. Stefano found it. He was going to have it fixed and give it back to her, but then he forgot about it with everything else going on. It was after she left for Germany that he noticed I was wearing the yellow one just like the blue one he had found. He asked about it."

"Why wouldn't he have known about them before?" Sarina asked.

"That was Luc," Valentina said. "She kept certain things between just the two of us."

Valentina studied the necklaces before she continued. "Anyway, I asked for it and had it fixed. I wore both necklaces for the longest time and when I went to visit Luc in Germany, I tried to give hers back to her. But she insisted I keep both."

"Why?" Sarina asked.

"Well," Valentina explained. "She said it would only remind her of what happened that night. But for me, they would remind me of her. So, I kept them."

Sarina reached out and fingered the delicate flow- on each chain.

How lost and in pain you must have been, Mama, to give up such a sentimental thing as a homage to a great friendship. Sarina's shoulders slumped forward, and she closed her eyes. *I promise I will find out what happened, Mama. I promise I will find out the truth.*

Valentina gathered all the pictures and the precious keepsakes and placed them back in the box. She led Sarina back downstairs and out into the garden. Antonio was nowhere in sight, but Stefano was still sitting in his chair sipping his coffee. Valentina freshened Sarina's coffee and while Sarina took her first sip, she noticed Valentina slip back into the house.

Sarina looked over her mug at Stefano and noticed he was staring out at the sea. He was so quiet and seemed so lost in thought that she was surprised when he spoke. "My son has told me that you wanted to talk with me."

She wondered if he was upset with her. *Perhaps this is a mistake.* But she was resolved to unravel the mystery, for her mother's sake, and decided to forge ahead with what she was sure would be a difficult conversation. "I'm sorry if it pains you to talk about this but I have to find peace for my mother. A peace she could never find."

Stefano turned his head to look at her. "Well, let's talk."

"I would like to know what happened—that night—from your point of view," Sarina said. "My grandmother told me what she knew but you are the one who found her. So—what happened? What did you see?"

"She was in a mood that night. We had argued on and off that day, but she was also excited about the festival." Stefano frowned. "She had been stomping grapes all day, so was thrilled about the prospect of what the harvest would bring that year for the winery. She was profoundly devoted to that place back then."

Stefano paused as though he were trying to figure out how to continue. "We went to the festival together. And even though we had argued earlier, we laughed, we danced, we ate food, and we drank wine. It had started out well. Then something happened and we started arguing again."

He looked back out toward the sea. "I can't even remember what we were arguing about, but she was so upset with me that she said she was going to go back to the vineyard instead of staying with me. That night was supposed to be when we made love for the first time. Silly I know to plan it, but we had decided it was time to commit to one another fully."

Stefano cleared his throat. "Sorry, you as her daughter probably don't want to hear that part."

"It's okay," Sarina said.

"I was also going to ask her to marry me that night," he said. "I had a ring in my pocket and when she stomped off, I thought about throwing it at her and telling her I wouldn't marry her now."

An expression of pain flitted across Stefano's face before he continued. "But I didn't. We could kiss, boy could we kiss and make out, and we would laugh for hours but, wow could we fight." His expression softened as he looked down at his coffee. "There was a passion there between us that never died even in the heat of an argument which sometimes fueled it the wrong way."

Sarina laughed, shifted in her seat, and frowned. "So, what happened?"

"Valentina walked by with a guy she was seeing at the time, and she noticed I was upset and asked me what was wrong. I told her Luc and I had argued, and she told me I was an idiot and that I should be chasing after her. After all, that was what Luc wanted and how did I not know this about Luc yet ..." He trailed off.

Sarina watched as Stefano's face brightened and he laughed. "Men are stupid."

"What?" Sarina asked.

"Valentina said men are stupid, while throwing her arms in the air," he explained, gesturing as Valentina must have gestured. "And she told me to run after

Luc. So, I ran after Luc in the same direction I had seen her stomp off earlier."

His smile faded and he looked back out at the sea. "The sound of the festival began to fade the further away I got. I could still hear a distant buzz of it all, but then I heard something else." He paused, staring at his hands. "It was a scream and all I could think was, oh god what had I done by letting her go off alone. I heard feet shuffling and as I turned the corner of the street, I saw Luc stand from a crouching position holding a knife. She looked dazed and lost and—there was—so much—blood."

Stefano wiped a tear away. "She had blood running down the side of her face and on the back of her head. Her lip was swollen, and she had scratches and bruises on her arms and legs. The dress she was wearing was torn at the bodice and down the right side, leaving her leg bare."

Sarina's head was buzzing at the description and Stefano looked as though he was struggling to continue before saying, "As I approached, she almost turned on me, but she recognized it was just me. She dropped the knife and collapsed in my arms. I picked her up and carried her to the nearest house where people were home, and we called the police. It took a while, but we tracked down her family and they met us at the doctor's home.

"We all asked her what happened. Together as a group, individually, everything, but all she could remember was Bernado was there, then everything was a blur. I asked her if Marco was there too, but she said she couldn't remember."

Stefano stopped as though to catch his breath. He looked at Sarina with so much sadness it took her breath away. "I wish to this day that I could have helped her more, but I didn't know what to do and there isn't a day that goes by that I regret not loving her and giving her time. Don't misunderstand, I love my wife, and I love the life I have but—"

"But you also love my mom," Sarina said.

"Yes." Stefano nodded. "And I regret not being able to help her find peace."

"Perhaps you would never have been able to give her peace even if she had stayed, and you were able to give her what she needed," Sarina said. "Perhaps it was always better this way and meant to be."

Stefano smiled. "That is what Sara said the day before I married Valentina."

"She is a wise woman, my great-grandmother. Perhaps you should listen to her."

"Yes, you are probably right." Stefano's smile faded and he looked out at the sea once more. "I just wish that we could find out what really happened that night. A lot of people think she killed Bernado but what possible motive could she have." He looked back at Sarina. "Plus, she wasn't that type of person. She was too tenderhearted and had too much respect for life to kill another human being. But still, the town of course had the rumors flying about and Bernado's father, well, he has never let go of the grudge he has toward your mother and her family."

"And now me," she said.

"And now you," he agreed.

"This Marco that everyone talks about, he was Bernado's best friend, right?" Sarina asked.

"Yes, he was," Stefano said.

"I know people questioned him, but he said the two went their separate ways earlier in the evening, correct?"

"That's right.

"Do you think he could be lying to protect something Bernado had done before the attack?" Sarina asked.

"It's possible, but the police questioned him, and he stuck to his story," Stefano said.

"Do you remember the shadows of that night?" Sarina asked, trying to think of anything that might help.

"What do you mean?"

"The shadows. Could they have been a silhouette of another individual running away?"

Stefano appeared to contemplate her question. "I don't know. I guess I never thought of that."

"Oh well, it was just a thought. I'm grasping at straws," Sarina said.

"No, it's okay," Stefano said.

Having another thought, she asked, "Could you show me where it happened?"

Stefano looked like he was surprised by her question and said that he would like to show her, but he didn't have time that day. "But I could have Antonio show you."

Sarina nodded and wondered if it was that he couldn't go or just wouldn't go. She figured it was the latter but wouldn't push it.

"Stefano," Sarina said, after the two sat in silence. "I can't imagine how difficult this was for you, but I want to tell you that I appreciate this, and I know my mother is smiling down from heaven knowing that we are working together to help find her peace at last."

Stefano thanked her for trying to find peace for his lost love. He stood and said, "I think I need a few minutes after remembering so much. Please excuse me."

Sarina rose and watched him walk away. Before he reached the house he paused and said, "I wish you luck on finding her peace," and disappeared into the house.

Sarina walked over to the edge of the garden and stared out at the sea. She heard someone approach from behind, turned her head and grinned when she saw it was Antonio.

"Are you okay?" he asked.

"Yes," Sarina said, "I am, for once, not a ball of emotions."

"I'm glad to hear you are okay," Antonio said and pulled her into a hug.

Antonio held her like she was a precious gift, kissed the top of her head and said, "Well, should we go see that spot, then head to the villa?"

Sarina nodded and looked up at Antonio. They stared into each other's eyes and she could feel the heat between them.

Antonio enveloped her into a long kiss and as they pulled apart, he said, "You have such strength, my love."

Sarina smiled. "I think my mother must be giving it to me."

"Perhaps, but I think a lot of it comes from within you," he said.

They walked hand in hand back into the house, where they found Valentina cleaning coffee mugs. Sarina said goodbye and Valentina rushed over to hug her. As the two women pulled apart Valentina said, "It was so lovely having you here."

"Thank you," Sarina said. "And thank you for sharing so many memories with me."

"It was my pleasure, Sarina," Valentina said.

Sarina and Antonio said their goodbyes again and left. Sarina had settled in the car to leave when Valentina came running out of the house toward them. Sarina opened her window as the woman stopped on her side of the car. Valentina handed the multicolored scarf from earlier to her. "You should have this, my dear."

"I couldn't," Sarina said.

"Yes, you could. And you should. It was mine only to keep for a little while. And now it belongs to the one who should have it."

Sarina hugged the scarf to her chest. "Thank you."

"You are most welcome, sweet Sarina."

As Sarina started to roll her window back up, she heard Valentina call, "Tell Sara that we will be there for dinner—ciao."

Antonio squeezed Sarina's hand. "Ready?"

"I am."

He put the car into gear and drove away. Sarina could see Valentina watching them leave in the side mirror and her thoughts began to wander to the discussions from earlier that morning. She shifted in her seat, looked ahead, and tried to stifle the dread that crept in with the swirl of thoughts, the closer they got to ... the spot.

Chapter Fifteen

Sarina stared at the street, surprised it was so quiet and peaceful. She wasn't sure what she'd expected to see but it wasn't a clean and serene roadway. There were a couple of corners where someone could have hidden in wait for a victim, but very few. For the most part it was an open spot.

"This is it," Antonio said.

Sarina stood over the spot where Bernado's body had been found and wondered how her mother must have felt standing in this same spot so many years before. Only this time the blood was long gone and there were only bits of dust and dirt from the roadway.

Could she have killed him?

"There is no way," Sarina said out loud.

Antonio took a step closer to Sarina. "No way for what?"

Sarina cleared her throat. "I was just thinking about my mother and how she must have felt standing here over his body. And ... and ..."

"And you wondered if she could have done it," he said.

Sarina's shoulders slumped forward, and she nodded her head. "Yes, but there is no way she could have. At least not willingly."

"We all agree with you, Sarina," Antonio said.

Could Bernado have been the one to attack my mother? Is it possible she did kill him on accident in the scuffle? Sarina shivered at the direction of her thoughts.

"Are you cold, Sarina?" Antonio asked.

"No, I was thinking about things and it unnerved me," she said.

She started to ask him about Bernado's character, but stopped when she noticed Marco walking in their direction. He seemed distracted and appeared to be upset. He neared the area where Sarina and Antonio stood, and he seemed to struggle with looking in their direction. When Marco lifted his face, he flinched, and Sarina realized Marco hadn't known she was there until that second.

"Hello, Marco," Sarina said. "Would you have a minute to maybe talk?"

"What are you doing?" Antonio whispered to Sarina.

"I want to talk to him, see if he can tell me anything," she whispered back.

"The police have already done that and came up with nothing, Sarina," he said.

"I know but ..." Sarina trailed off.

Antonio sighed. "Go ahead, but he may not talk to you."

Sarina took a step toward Marco. "Marco, is it okay if we talk?"

"Just leave me alone," Marco yelled. He stood like he was rooted to the ground, so Sarina took another step toward him.

"Please," Sarina said. "I just have a few questions."

"No," Marco yelled. "Just. Leave. Me. Alone."

Sarina stopped walking. "I'm sorry, I don't mean to upset you. I just want to find out what happened."

Marco's eyes widened even more, he turned and ran back the way he'd come.

Sarina tried to run after him. "Please Marco, I just want to talk."

"Sarina, it's no use," Antonio called.

Marco came to a corner up the street and paused. He took one look at Sarina, a look flashed across his face that reminded her of guilt, and he disappeared around the corner.

"He knows something," Sarina said. She continued to run up the street toward where Marco had disappeared.

"Sarina, please," Antonio called from behind her. "It's no use."

She stopped running, stared at the empty sidewalk where Marco had fled. She turned back toward Antonio who caught up to her and wrapped his arms around her.

"Are you okay?" he asked.

"Marco knows something," she said. "He is hiding something. I can tell."

"You could tell this by the way he ran away?" Antonio asked.

"No, I could tell by the look of guilt on his ashen face," Sarina said.

Antonio kissed the top of her head. "Hmm, maybe you are right."

"Do you think I am wrong, Gigi?" Sarina asked her great-grandmother.

Sarina had explained the encounter with Marco and her great-grandmother had not responded yet. Gigi appeared to be studying her, so Sarina asked again. "Do you think I could be wrong?"

"No, not necessarily," Gigi said. "But tread carefully, dear. It is one thing to accuse a man who is guilty but another to accuse a man who is innocent."

"Do you think he is innocent?" Sarina asked. "Or at least being truthful?"

"Truthful—innocent—perhaps not," Gigi said. "But I care for your safety. When one carries a burden of guilt and a secret for this long, then one will do anything to protect themselves, including harming others who may be figuring out the truth."

"I see," Sarina said. "So, this could potentially be a little dangerous, especially if there was more to what happened than what we thought."

"I think so," Gigi said.

"I will be careful, I promise," Sarina said. "I will always have someone with me while I try to figure things out."

Gigi nodded. "I will hold you to your promise. Now please excuse me, my dear, I need to finish preparations for our dinner this evening."

As Gigi started to walk inside Sarina remembered her ledger concerns. "Is Uncle Tobias around today?"

Gigi stopped and appeared puzzled by the question. "He is in Florence until next weekend visiting some friends. Is there anything I can help with?"

"No, it's okay," Sarina said. "It can wait. I had a couple of questions that's all. Just trying to figure out a few more things."

"If you're sure," her great-grandmother said.

"Of course. Thank you though," Sarina said. "Well, I will let you get back to dinner preparations I need to go find Sofia anyway."

Stefano and Valentina arrived right on time for dinner. They were soon followed by Sarina's grandparents. Sarina was worried Stefano might still be upset over the conversation she had with him earlier that day, but she soon found the sorrow in Stefano's eyes had been replaced by his usual twinkle.

Aunt Gianna and her family were already at the villa, minus Tito; he had volunteered to work at the restaurant that night so that Alessandro could attend the special dinner. Georgio the second, Arturo, and their families arrived soon after Stefano and Valentina.

Sarina watched everyone mingle. *So, it appears the whole family was invited tonight.*

Alfonso sat in a corner drinking a beverage and appeared to be sulking. Sarina knew he'd had a meeting with the businessmen earlier that day, and she wondered if things had not gone as well as he had hoped. She meant to ask him about it earlier, but had not had the chance. Now was not the time. A few more of her cousins were coming in from the vineyard and wine barn, and they were washing up for dinner.

Antonio was the last to come in and he looked concerned. Sarina noticed his expression and hoped it wasn't because of the incident with Marco earlier that day. He scanned the room and walked over to Sarina when he spied her. She glanced around the room to see if anyone was watching. But Antonio shrugged as though to say, what the hell, and pulled Sarina in for a kiss. When he let go, she heard an onslaught of whistles and teasing. Sarina's face grew hot, and she laughed.

"Oh, that is enough of the teasing," Gigi hollered above the noise. "Come let's go eat."

The group quieted, made their way to the courtyard, and scattered around the table. If anyone had been watching Sarina and Antonio on their way to the table, they would have noticed Antonio whisper in her ear and Sarina whisper something in return.

Alfonso sat next to Sarina, leaned over, and whispered, "Is something the matter, dear cousin?"

Sarina flinched at the sneer, recovered, and smiled sweetly. "Not at all. Antonio had a question and I set him at ease."

"I see, well let me know if I can help in any way," Alfonso said.

"Thank you, but I think we are okay," she said.

Sarina shuddered, but forced herself to focus on dinner.

An hour later the dinner group gathered around the fire pit.

Sarina stepped away from the group to refill her wine and Alfonso pulled her aside.

"Look, I am sorry if I was rude earlier okay," Alfonso said. "It's just been a long day. And the meeting with the businessmen didn't go as well as I hoped it would. They are trying to manipulate things and I am frustrated with the whole thing."

"Is there a way I can help?" Sarina asked.

"Well," Alfonso said, "maybe you can join me on Tuesday for a lunch with them in Grosseto."

"I'm so sorry, Alfonso," Sarina said, "I am busy Tuesday, so I can't." Sarina wasn't so busy she couldn't rearrange her schedule to join Alfonso, but something about the meeting and the businessmen made her uncomfortable.

"Pity," Alfonso said, "Jarrod Fraser will miss you."

Sarina glared at him and walked away. She could hear Alfonso laughing at her as she disappeared into the kitchen to get more wine. When she returned to the fire, she sat next to Antonio.

The family played music, sang songs, and told stories. After a lull of conversation and loud music, Nonna stood. "Now that everyone is here. I have something to say." She paused and took a breath. "Our wonderful Luc has passed on, but she has sent us her Sarina—who is now our Sarina."

Nonna smiled at her. "Sarina has brought Luc to us in the only way she could. She brought Luc's ashes. We must help Sarina figure out a time and a place for Luc to be at rest at last. I will let you all know when that time has come and where it will be, but if you have suggestions, please let me know."

A hush fell over the group as Nonna sat back down. Sarina felt compelled to say something next, since everyone was glancing at her.

She stood and cleared her throat. "Thank you, Nonna, for letting everyone know about my mother's ashes." Sarina paused and looked around. Her hands began to shake when she saw everyone looking back at her.

She took a deep breath. "It was her wish to have them laid to rest here, and she asked me to find a place for her to be at peace. I don't feel right about doing it yet, though. Maybe it is because there is unfinished business that needs to be resolved before I feel right about it. I need to know for sure. I need to close that awful chapter in her life. Then maybe she will truly be at peace once and for all."

Antonio squeezed Sarina's hand and she looked down at him and smiled. She looked at the fire and stared into it while it danced about.

"I didn't know the life my mama had here," Sarina continued. "Or the family, and friends, she had. And I didn't know the pain she endured but as I learn more and more, I can't let it go. I have to try and find out more. I know this isn't easy for you all, but I believe with all my heart that I must do this. Then perhaps all our hearts will heal, and the past will finally be laid to rest."

Sarina sat and worried about the stillness that fell over the group. She wondered if she had overstepped a line somewhere, but her Uncle Arturo put her mind at ease.

"I think it is brave of you to take on such a challenge," Uncle Arturo said, "and I pray you help her, and the family find some resolution in this."

Sarina nodded but noticed he had tears in eyes. Sarina glanced around at everyone else and noticed other eyes were filled with moisture as well.

Gigi, the matriarch of the family, stood. "Enough of speeches. It is time for drink." She called for the housekeeper and whispered something in her ear. The housekeeper nodded and went into the house.

When she returned, she had several bottles of wine that Sarina had not seen before. The housekeeper opened a bottle and handed it to Gigi. Gigi lifted the bottle in the air. "This is Luc's wine. It was the special wine she created that year. As most of you know, we have not had any of it, but I believe we should drink some now in Luc's honor, and in honor of her daughter coming home to us. We will not drink any again until Luc is laid to rest and at peace at last."

Glasses were filled with the special wine. Gigi raised her glass in the air—"Salute"—and drank her wine.

"Salute," was the responding chorus and everyone drank.

Sarina's eyebrows raised and she smiled at the special flavoring of the wine. It was the best glass of wine she had ever tasted. She started to ask what was in it, but her great-grandmother answered the question for her.

"Luc created the recipe for this special wine, and she didn't share it with anyone else that we are aware of. If she shared it with anyone, then I pray they someday come forward so we can add this to our wines and continue to make it in her honor. It is indeed special just as Luc was."

The rest of the evening was a solemn one and as the group started to disperse Sarina yawned and her eyes grew heavy. The exhaustion of the emotional roller coaster of her day had caught up with her.

"You should run on to bed, Sarina," Antonio said.

"I think I might. I am so tired all of a sudden," she said.

"I will be back on Monday. You should rest tomorrow," Antonio said. "You had a full day today and could use it."

She smiled. "Yes, I think a day of rest would be wise."

They walked hand in hand to Antonio's car. Once there, Antonio pulled Sarina into a deep kiss. When they parted he said, "Good night, Sarina."

"Good night, Antonio," she said.

He pulled her into one last kiss, sighed, climbed into his car, and left.

As Sarina waved goodbye to him, Nonna walked up behind her and put an arm around her. "Be careful of your heart and his, my dear. Until you decide your future, it is not wise to create something that cannot be, especially without decisions made."

Sarina looked at her grandmother. "I know. It's just that I am so drawn to him."

"Yes, as your mother was drawn to his father, but it was not meant to be in the end."

Sarina nodded, hugged her grandmother, and whispered, "I love you, Nonna."

"Oh," Nonna gasped. "And I you, Sarina."

They turned and walked arm in arm into the house.

Chapter Sixteen

*T*oday is the day, Sarina thought, as she bounded out of bed. She was determined to start digging deeper into her mother's past and today was the day she was going to visit the police station. Sarina got dressed and went in search of Sofia to see if she would have some free time to take her into the village.

It was the Wednesday after speaking with Stefano and Sarina couldn't stop thinking about all he had shared. Sarina's determination had grown every day since speaking with him and she wouldn't put things off any longer.

Sarina found Sofia in the kitchen making coffee.

"Good morning, Sofia," Sarina said.

Sofia turned and her face brightened. "Good morning."

"Would you be able to take me into the village today? And drop me off at the police station?"

Sofia almost dropped her mug and placed it on the counter. "Hmm—the police station?"

"Yes, I want to ask some questions about my mother's case."

Sofia appeared to be studying Sarina before saying," Are you sure you want to do this?"

"I know what you're thinking. And I know everyone is worried about what I might discover. But I have to know. I just have to ..." Sarina trailed off.

Sofia poured the now brewed coffee into two mugs and handed one to Sarina. "Okay, if you are sure you want to do this. I know I can't stop you. And neither should anyone else. Just be prepared for the possibility of not finding what you want to find."

Sarina grinned. "I know. Thank you."

"Of course," Sofia said. "I have to run a few items to my brothers' restaurant. I will drop you on the way. Is that okay?"

"That works."

"Okay, when can you be ready to go?"

"I am ready now," Sarina said.

"Ha—okay. Give me five minutes and I will be ready," Sofia said.

"That sounds great. I will go grab my purse, and meet you at your truck," Sarina said.

"See you in a few minutes."

Sarina ran back up to her room, grabbed her purse and ran out to meet Sofia at the truck. Sarina arrived at the truck first, but she didn't have to wait long for Sofia and they drove out of the villa toward town.

"I talked with Leone," Sofia said.

"How did that go?"

"He said he was feeling the same as me. He wanted to make more of a commitment with me but wasn't sure how I was feeling about things, so was hesitant to say anything," Sofia explained.

"I think that is wonderful, Sofia," Sarina said. "Have you shared any of this with your mother yet?"

"Yes and no," Sofia said. "I am not trying to keep things from her, just haven't had a lot of time together just the two of us."

"How do you think your family will react?"

"My mother, sisters, and Tito will be excited for me, but my father and Alessandro will be a little more protective. At least they will pretend to be anyway," Sofia said.

"Well, I am excited for you,'" Sarina said.

"Thanks for giving me the advice to talk to him."

They talked about Leone and Sofia's date with him later that week. They laughed when Sarina asked questions and Sofia would blush. Soon Sofia stopped in front of an old brick building that looked like it had seen better days. It was still sound in structure, but it appeared to not have had a lot of updates over the years.

Sarina climbed out of the truck while the two agreed she would meet Sofia at the restaurant when she was done. Sarina waved as Sofia drove off. She turned around, took a deep breath—"Here goes noth-ing"—and walked into the police station.

She paused inside the door to allow her eyes to ad-just and heard activity—a phone ringing, people talking quietly, the whir of the copy machine. Sarina cleared her throat, took another deep breath, and walked to what she believed was the front desk of-ficer, or whatever he was called.

It took her a few minutes to explain why she was there before she was ushered back to an office and of-fered something to drink. Sarina declined. The officer nodded his head and left.

Sarina looked around the office to pass the time. *It looks like I walked on to an old movie set of an interrogation room.* She sat at a dull wooden table and her chair squeaked every time she moved. A plant in the corner looked as though it hadn't been watered in some time. The walls were an ugly slate gray color. Sarina was surprised to see a large bulletin board along one wall with various flyers and wanted posters.

This must be a conference room of sorts instead of the in-terrogation room. Sarina smiled at her imagination as an officer who looked to be in his forties bustled into the room. He greeted Sarina with sincerity and ex-pressed his sympathy at her mother's passing. He explained he had known her mother as they had gone to school together. After a few minutes of discussing the way things used to be, he finally asked how he could help her.

She swallowed and took a deep breath. "Well—you see—um—I would like to see the files on my mother's case."

"I'm not sure we can do that," he explained.

"Why not?" Sarina asked. "I want to find out what happened, and it seems like a good place to start."

The officer studied Sarina as though he were trying to figure out how to proceed. He nodded his head, like he had made up his mind about something, excused himself, and left the office. A few minutes later he returned with a box.

"There isn't much in here, Sarina," the officer said, "but you can look through it if you would like."

She thanked him and started to look through the contents of the box. Sarina picked up a sealed plastic bag that contained her mother's torn dress, stained with blood. "Was a DNA test ever run on any of this?" she asked.

"Of course," the officer said, "but the only thing we found was your mother's blood and the deceased's blood."

"How much of the case do you know?" Sarina asked. She pulled out the file folder and thumbed through the documents. She paused when she saw Marco's name on one of the reports. She separated it from the stack and stared at it with frustration at not being able to read it.

"I was not in the force back then," he said, "but my father led the case. He was pretty upset about the whole thing as your mother's family is well respected. He also wanted to find something to help calm your mother, I think. She was haunted by demons of that night that is for sure."

Sarina glanced at the officer over the report. Looking back at the report, her eyebrows furrowed, and she squinted but all she could read was Marco's name. She had picked up a few words here and there since her time in Italy but was not fluent enough to be able to decipher a police report.

She held out the report toward the officer. "This is a report on the interview from Marco, right. Can you tell me what it says?"

"That one is a mystery about that night," the officer said.

"What do you mean?" Sarina asked.

"Well, I probably shouldn't be telling you this, but my father always felt like Marco knew more than what he was telling us," he said.

"Why didn't he do anything about it?" Sarina asked.

"He did," the officer explained. "He held him in a cell for a couple of days, but the man didn't change his story. At one point Marco apparently broke down, cried, and said he just wanted to go home and grieve for his lost friend. My father had no choice but to let him go."

"Whose knife was at the scene?" she asked.

"That is a mystery too. We don't know," the officer said.

"There are no clues at all?" Sarina asked.

"It wasn't your mother's knife, according to your family," the officer said. "And when my father asked Aldo if he recognized it, he said it was not his son's knife. According to my father though, the way he said it was kind of odd. My father worked on this case for long hours and never developed any new leads. If he had come up with one witness or if your mother had remembered what happened, then it would have been helpful."

"Did your father or the police department ever suspect my mother of killing him?" Sarina asked.

"No, not even once," he said. "My father never thought for a moment that she could, not intentionally anyway. But he had to question her anyway. Aldo swore she killed his son but had no proof."

"Why was he so sure she killed him?"

"Aldo said it was because her fingerprints were on the knife," the officer explained. "Which they were, but my father didn't remember telling him this.

Which brings us back to Marco, and why my father thought he might have been there for at least part of it anyway or saw what happened to them and got spooked—something—but he never would talk."

"Do Marco and Aldo still talk?" Sarina asked.

"All the time. They fish together," the office said. "And Marco helps take care of Aldo. Aldo has no one. His wife passed away when their son was a child and he never remarried. He is kind of a gruff man though, so it would be difficult for him to find someone who would put up with him." The officer's face turned red. "My apologies. That was uncalled for and unprofessional."

"It's okay," Sarina said. She studied everything in front of her and asked, "What do you think happened?"

"I don't know, but I have found that sometimes the past is best left in the past," he said. "You may find out that what happened was far worse than what we could imagine and could paint an image of your mother you don't want to see. I have seen that happen before and it very well could be that it's best to just let this lie where it is."

"Maybe," Sarina mumbled. She nodded toward the report on Marco that the officer still held. "Can you tell me what the report actually says about Marco's interview?" she asked one final time.

The policeman studied the report. "Nothing really. But in summary it states that the questions were asked such as, where was he, did he see anything suspicious, was there anyone out to get either one of them, and so on. He had the perfect answers for each question. He said he wasn't there, he didn't know what happened, and he was not aware of anyone wanting to cause either of them harm."

Sarina nodded and realized she'd discovered what she thought she would by coming here—nothing. But she had to try anyway. She gathered her things and started to walk out of the room. She paused. "Thank you for your time and thank you for sharing all of this with me."

"I was happy to help but remember what I said. Sometimes the past is best left in the past."

Sarina thanked him a second time and walked out.

She walked down the street toward her cousins' restaurant. She was so deep in thought, she almost missed the man barreling down on her. Sarina jumped out of the way. When the man started to walk past her, Sarina tried to stop him. "Aldo Bianchi, please sir, I would like to talk with you, just for a minute or two."

"I have nothing to say to you," Aldo said and kept walking.

She followed Aldo and tried to ask more questions, but he continued to stomp up the street. Sarina stopped and threw up her arms. "Don't you want to find out what really happened to your son?"

Aldo stopped and spun around. Sarina flinched and took a step back when she saw the look on his face. He shortened the distance between them. Sarina shrunk back as Aldo loomed over her. He was quiet except for his deep breathing as he stared down at Sarina. When Sarina thought he wasn't going to say anything he took another step forward. "I know what happened. Your mother killed him." Aldo swung around and started to stomp away.

"But how do you know that is really what happened?" Sarina asked as she followed Aldo. "She was attacked too, remember."

Aldo reeled around. "Was it that she was attacked, or was he fighting her off?"

"You can't seriously believe that, sir," Sarina said with a snort. "Your son, I was told, was twice the size as my mother."

"How dare you laugh at this," Aldo yelled.

"I'm not laughing at the situation sir, but you have to admit that what you are proposing is laughable," Sarina said. "My mother could no more have killed your son the way you are claiming then I would be able to kill you."

"Are you threatening me?"

"Of course not," Sarina snapped. She took a deep breath, tried to calm her pounding heart and said, "I am merely making a point."

"Well, go point out things to someone else and leave me alone," he said.

"Fine. I will," Sarina said. "Do you know where I can find Marco?"

"You leave that boy alone," Aldo said. "He has gone through enough."

"Perhaps you are right, but I want to find out what happened," Sarina said. "I will follow up with Marco. Have a good day, sir."

She turned and started to walk away when she heard footsteps stomping behind her. Aldo grabbed her arm and spun her around. He shoved her against the side of a building, grabbed the front of her clothes, and lifted her into the air. Her legs dangled and Sarina tried to free herself.

"Put me down," Sarina snapped. "You're hurting me."

"You leave this alone or you and your family will be sorry. Do you hear me?" Aldo yelled, inches from her face.

He was shouting loud enough people started to gather on the street. A shop owner who came out to investigate the noise came to Sarina's rescue. The shop keeper pulled her from Aldo's grasp and asked if she was okay. She nodded, thanked the shop keeper, and ran in the opposite direction toward her cousins' restaurant. She could hear Aldo yelling curses and threats behind her, but she didn't slow down until she rounded a corner out of sight.

Sarina stopped and leaned against the side of a building. She rested her trembling hand on her chest, took deep breaths, and tried to steady her racing heart. She believed she hit a nerve today with Aldo, and that the nerve was Marco. *There is something there that we are missing with Marco and Aldo. Maybe they are protecting Bernado.*

Sarina took one more deep breath, pulled away from the building, and walked the rest of the way to her cousins' restaurant. By the time she arrived at the restaurant, she was calm.

Movement at the boat dock caught Sarina's attention, and she squinted, not believing her eyes. Marco was walking up the boat dock. She took off running toward the docks. When Marco saw her, he turned around and ran back to his boat. He threw the lines into his boat, started its engine, and steered it out toward the sea.

Sarina ran as fast as she could, but when she got to the edge of the dock, Marco's boat was too far away.

"Please, Marco, I just want to know the truth," Sarina yelled. "And I believe you know what it is."

Marco shifted his body so she could see his face. He appeared pale and Sarina couldn't tell if his expression read anger, alarm, or a mixture of the two.

Sarina threw her arms in the air when Marco didn't say anything. "Fine," Sarina mumbled and gave up. For now.

When Sarina started to walk away, Marco yelled, "Leave me alone. I told Aldo about you bothering me and he doesn't like it. You should watch yourself."

She shuddered and continued walking toward the shoreline and her cousins' restaurant.

"Sarina, are you okay?" Sofia called from the sidewalk close to the restaurant entrance.

Sarina looked toward her and asked, "Where did you come from?"

"I got worried since you were gone so long so I went up to the police station. And you didn't answer my question. Are you okay?"

"Yes, I'm okay," Sarina said. "Rough morning but I'm fine."

"Really? Because I heard about Aldo threatening you and the family. I saw the interaction between you and Marco. Are you sure you're okay?"

"Actually, no. I think I could use a drink and I am pretty sure Aldo bruised my arm," Sarina said.

"We should file a police report and get a protection order against him, do something."

"Is that like a restraining order? If we do that then I may not be able to talk to him or question him again. And I may not be able to question Marco," Sarina said.

"You can't be serious," Sofia said.

Sarina reached Sofia and Sofia hugged her. When they pulled apart Sofia said, "You must have a death wish."

"No, I just want to find out the truth."

Sofia nodded and they walked into the restaurant. Alessandro walked over to them when they entered and asked what food he could bring them. Sofia waved off her brother's suggestion of food and said, "Food can wait. We need a drink."

Alessandro's eyebrows raised. "What's wrong? What happened?"

Sofia patted his arm. "I will explain later, but for now let's get Sarina a drink."

"Okay," Alessandro said. He steered them to the bar, ordered two of the house drink specials and excused himself to go make them something to eat.

Sofia made sure Sarina was okay before following Alessandro into the kitchen. Sarina sat at the bar sipping her beverage. She was lost in thought of the morning's events and didn't notice when a man sat next to her.

"Well, if it isn't the pretty American from Iowa who doesn't speak a lick of Italian."

Sarina jolted, looked over at the stranger, and forced her thoughts to the present. She blinked at the man and tried to reason how she knew him.

"Please tell me you know who I am. If you don't my ego will be forever bruised," the man said.

Sarina blinked again and remembered. "I doubt that, Mr. Fraser."

"So, you do remember me," Jarrod Fraser said. "Hopefully, it is a fond memory."

Sarina rolled her eyes and looked back at her drink. "I'm sorry, Mr. Fraser, but I am not the best company right now."

"Please call me Jarrod. Trouble in paradise, my sweet?"

Sarina bristled and shook her head. "No, my paradise is fine." Thinking of Antonio, Sarina's heart skipped a beat, and she felt her expression soften. "Actually, my paradise is wonderful."

"I must say that saddens me," Jarrod said. "I was hoping you and I could have some paradise of our own." Jarrod put his arm around Sarina's waist. She flinched and pulled away, then stood and moved to another bar stool.

"So, you are playing hard to get I see," Jarrod said and moved next to her.

"Look, Mr. Fraser," she snapped. "I don't really want to be rude, but I have had a long day already and I am not in the mood for someone like you. Now if you wouldn't mind leaving me alone, that would be great."

Jarrod blinked at her and had a look on his face like he couldn't believe she was giving him the brush off. He cleared his throat. "I must be losing my touch. Surely you just need to spend some more time with me."

Jarrod reached out toward her again when Tito came out of nowhere and stood beside her. "Is this guy bothering you, Sarina?"

Sarina wanted to say yes but she didn't want to ruin Alfonso's business deal since things were up in the air already, so she shook her head and said, "No, Mr. Fraser was just leaving to join his business partner and was saying an overly friendly farewell."

Tito stared Jarrod down until Jarrod backed away a step. Tito cleared his throat and said, "Perhaps you should go ahead and join your business partner and leave my cousin be."

Jarrod appeared to be sizing up Tito and the situation. After a tense moment he laughed and bowed slightly to Sarina. "Until we meet again, beautiful lady."

After he left, Tito turned to meet Sarina's gaze. "I'm sorry. I wish I would have had the chance to come over sooner."

"It's okay, Tito," she said. "It's just been a rough day."

"So I've heard," he said. "Perhaps after your drink and something to eat you should head back to the villa. Get some rest."

Sarina nodded and her eyes misted.

Tito's whole countenance softened as he said, "Aww, don't cry. I can't stand a woman's tears."

She laughed. "I'm sorry, cousin. I am just feeling emotional."

"Of course, Sarina, of course," Tito said.

A few seconds later, Sofia walked out from the kitchen with two plates and set them on the bar in front of Sarina. She looked from Sarina to Tito and back to Sarina. "I leave you for five minutes and my stupid brother makes you cry." Sofia followed her statement up with a smack on Tito's shoulder.

"Ach, I did not make her cry," Tito said and rubbed his shoulder.

"Well, I don't see anyone else about," Sofia said.

Sarina laughed at Tito's pleading look and said, "It's okay, Sofia. He didn't make me cry. I think I am ready to head to the villa though."

"But we haven't eaten lunch yet."

"I don't think she feels much like eating now," Tito said.

"Did you hear what happened to her then?" Sofia asked him.

"Yes," he said.

Brother and sister exchanged worried glances. "Sarina, come, let's go home, yes?" Sofia asked.

"Yes," Sarina said.

"But we are taking the food to go," Sofia said.

The ride to the villa was a quiet one and Sarina stared out the window. She could tell Sofia wanted to ask questions about the morning's events but was thankful she refrained.

When Sofia turned in to the driveway of the villa, Sarina broke the silence. "Thank you for taking me into town. Perhaps you can do it again sometime next week."

"Sure, anything you need," Sofia responded with a smile. Sofia pulled the truck to an empty spot and parked. She turned to Sarina and said, "I hope you don't mind me saying something here. I know you have this need to find out the truth and I can only imagine what you must be feeling but—do you think perhaps it should be left—"

"Left alone?" Sarina finished for Sofia.

"Yes. I mean the way Aldo treated you and his threats. I worry for you and for the family," Sofia said.

Sarina nodded. "I know, I worry too, but the more I learn the more desperate I am to know the truth. Does that make any sense?"

Sofia nodded, reached over, and squeezed her cousin's hand. "It does make sense. And I support you no matter what. Just—please be careful, okay."

"I promise," Sarina said and crawled out of the truck.

Chapter Seventeen

Sarina decided not to go into town for a while after the incidents with Aldo, Marco, and Jarrod. She wanted to catch her breath before going at it again. Besides, it was close to harvest and things were getting busy at the vineyard. And she still wanted to figure out what was going on with the ledgers.

She studied the ledger, but was distracted by the memory of Antonio when he found out what had happened with Aldo, Marco, and Jarrod. Antonio had said he was going to show them a thing or two about mistreating a lady, but Sarina had stopped him with a kiss. Her body warmed at the memory of his lips on hers and the passion that soared between them.

A noise outside brought her back to the present and she focused on preparing her notes for when she could meet with her great-uncle. She was thankful she had finally caught up with him and they were scheduled to meet the next morning. Sarina hoped the meeting wouldn't get delayed.

It was getting later into the evening and Sarina knew she should go down and say goodnight to Gigi soon, but she wanted to finish her notes first. She stretched and jotted down a few more thoughts when Gigi poked her head in the door.

"Goodness, Sarina, you spend so much time poring over those books. I love your passion and your interest."

Sarina laughed. "I can't help it. I guess it's the accountant in me."

Gigi crossed the room and sat on the window seat across from the desk. They talked about the day's work and activities and started to discuss what needed to happen next to prepare for the harvest. It dawned on Sarina that she had been there for over a month and her great-grandmother would want an answer soon. But she wasn't ready to give one yet. She wasn't sure what held her back from committing to a life here and wondered if she was waiting for some sort of sign.

"Did you finally meet up with Tobia to discuss your questions?" Gigi broke into Sarina's thoughts.

"I plan to meet with him in the morning," Sarina said.

"Well, I hope you get the answers you need," her great-grandmother said.

"Me too," Sarina said as she stood to cross the room and get a closer look at something outside.

"Is something wrong? You seem distracted," Gigi said.

Sarina squinted. "Oh no." She ran out on to the balcony to get a better look. "Oh my god," she cried. "Fire!"

Gigi jumped from her seat and ran out to stand next to Sarina. Sarina didn't think about what she should do next, she just sprang into action. She ran through the house hollering, "Fire in the vineyard! Fire in the vineyard!"

People sprang out of their rooms, shouting and tripping over each other as they followed her outside. Some grabbed blankets, others grabbed buckets. Sarina snatched a water hose and dragged it as far as she could toward the fire. It wouldn't reach far enough, so she dropped the hose, grabbed a bucket, filled it with water and ran toward the blaze.

She quickly assessed the situation and saw that one of the outbuildings and the first row of vines were the only things burning. She wasn't sure what came over her as she took control of the situation. If they couldn't put the fire out quickly, it would spread to the rest of the vines.

"Okay, you guys start focusing on the vines," Sarina yelled. "Nicole, see if you can't get the hose I had closer somehow."

"On it," Nicole said.

Sarina looked around, saw the others working on putting the vines out, so she focused on the outbuilding. She didn't think as she ran into the building. Flames shot up the back wall and lapped at the ceiling above, and the haze of smoke made it difficult to see. She saw a few barrels of wine and ran to the first one. It wouldn't budge. She coughed and looked around. She spotted some tools and boards and tried to leverage them to force the barrel onto its side to roll it out, but she wasn't strong enough. The flames had spread to encompass half of the building, and they continued to inch closer while she worked on the barrel. She coughed and wheezed and decided to go get help. She ran outside screaming for assistance and was about to run back in when Sofia grabbed her from behind.

"Let it go. It's too dangerous."

Sarina turned her focus on the vines. She hollered for Nicole and Cosimo the third to get the water sprinkler system going and to run a second hose to the vines to put them out. She instructed Sofia to douse the other vines with water to hopefully prevent them from catching fire.

Sarina grabbed another bucket and ran back and forth from the water tank to the vines. She threw so many buckets of water on the blaze she thought for sure they should be making headway by now. But the fire continued to put up a fight.

In between throwing buckets of water, Sarina continued to bark orders to everyone until finally the first row of vines were a smoldering mass of ash and twisted charcoal. Sarina directed everyone to turn their attention to the outbuilding, but Sofia stopped her.

"It's no use. The building is gone. It's best now to just let it burn. We can't do any more."

"Okay, well let's at least douse the trees and everything around it so nothing else will catch fire," Sarina said.

"Good idea," Sofia agreed and relayed the message to the rest of the group.

Sarina helped the group finish the final chore of controlling the fire and watched while the flames consumed the outbuilding. Tears welled up in her eyes and she wondered at her emotions over a place she hadn't known existed several months before.

Gigi broke through the crowd and appeared to take in the scene. She nodded as though dismissing the vines as a loss and looked at Sarina. She seemed to read Sarina's expression because she walked over and pulled Sarina to her. "You did all you could, my child."

Gigi held Sarina while the two watched the fire die into a steaming pile of twisted wood and metal. Sarina pulled away from her great-grandmother, picked up another bucket full of water and directed the group to dump water on the dying embers to keep it from springing back to life.

The group focused all their energy on the embers until Cosimo the third confirmed the fire wouldn't be able to flare up. The group made their way back to the house and separated to their own rooms. Sarina glanced at a wall clock as she walked toward her room and noticed it was three in the morning.

Exhausted and grimy from the event, Sarina thought briefly about just falling into bed. She decided against it, went to her bathroom, and tried to turn on her shower before undressing, but the pressure was low since everyone else was trying to shower, too.

"I'm impressed at the way you took control," Gigi hollered from Sarina's bedroom. Hopefully, this tells you you are meant to lead."

Sarina turned off her shower and walked back into the bedroom. "Maybe. I was just so desperate to stop the fire and keep it from expanding. But I really don't know what came over me. I couldn't stand the thought of losing something else I guess."

"I know the feeling," Gigi said as she reached out and placed a gentle hand on Sarina's arm.

Sarina winced. She moved the torn sleeve to get a better look at her arm. Gigi gasped. An ugly burn ran along the length of her right forearm.

"The adrenalin you felt must have kept you from noticing your arm until now," Gigi said.

"I remember feeling some stings but didn't think anything about it."

Gigi nodded. "Go take a cool shower, and when you get out, I will wrap your wound.

Too tired to argue, Sarina went and turned on her shower and was thankful the pressure was better now. Sarina felt like she was moving in slow motion while she undressed and showered. It felt good to wash off the grime, but the burn grew more painful by the second until it stung, and she tried not to use her right arm.

When she got out of the shower, she carefully put on a tank top so as not to brush her arm, slid on pajama pants, and walked into her bedroom. She found Gigi had some salve, bandages, over-the-counter pain pills, and a glass of water.

"Come sit on the bed," Gigi said.

Sarina obeyed, and once she was comfortable, Gigi set about rubbing salve on the burn. Sarina flinched with every touch, but knew it was necessary. Once Sarina's arm was covered in salve and wrapped in a bandage, her great-grandmother helped her lie back in bed.

"Get some rest, Sarina," her great-grandmother said.

"I will try," Sarina said. "Good night, Gigi."

"Good night, Sarina." Gigi gathered the salve and left-over bandages and started to leave the room.

Sarina asked, "Do you believe the fire was set on purpose?"

Gigi paused. "Yes, I do. When I got on the scene, I thought I caught a whiff of gasoline."

"I thought so too," Sarina mumbled.

"I will call the police first thing tomorrow," her great-grandmother said.

"I think that's a good idea," Sarina said.

"And we might point in the direction of Aldo or Marco as possible suspects," Gigi said. "I know they threatened you."

"I wondered if it might be them too," Sarina said.

"Well let's not worry about that now, get some rest, Sarina."

Sarina woke in the morning to the sting in her arm. She winced as she sat up and forced the bile back down her throat. Sarina stumbled her way into the bathroom and found it difficult to move about her morning routine while her arm felt like it was in flames, but she made it work.

Once she completed her task, she felt stuck. She slumped against the sink and she thought she might be sick at the thought of taking another step. Sarina contemplated what to do when she heard a knock at her bedroom door.

"Is everything okay, Sarina?" Antonio called.

"In here," Sarina yelled.

Antonio walked in and she saw his expression change to what looked like panic. It only took seconds for him to recover, and he sprang into action.

"Okay," Antonio said, "We are going to take a towel and get it wet with cool water, wrap your arm with it, and get you back to bed. And then I am going to call the doctor."

Sarina nodded and allowed Antonio to take control. Once Antonio got her settled in bed, he dialed a number on his cell phone and spoke loudly and quickly in Italian to someone on the other line. After he disconnected the call, he turned to Sarina. "You just rest here. I am going to go get you a glass of water."

"Okay," she mumbled while Antonio rushed out of the room.

Sarina started to close her eyes when her door burst open. There was a flurry of activity as Gigi and the housekeeper came in to examine her wounds. Antonio rushed in with the glass of water, while Sofia hovered in the background. After Gigi's assessment of the burn, Sofia and Antonio were sent on errands to bring more water, salve, and bandages.

When the doctor arrived, he was rushed into Sarina's room. He inspected the wound and said a few things in Italian to Gigi. Sarina tried to figure out what the doctor was saying but gave up because he was talking too fast. He put a different salve on the burn and wrapped the arm again. He left a tube of the new salve next to Sarina's bed on her nightstand, along with some stronger pain medication. He instructed Sarina to keep her arm elevated and left.

Gigi turned to Sarina after the door closed and gingerly propped her arm on several pillows. "No need to worry. You will be fine, but you must rest today. Okay."

Sarina nodded and her eyes fluttered but sleep wouldn't come. Gigi pulled the covers up around her, double checked her arm was elevated enough and kissed Sarina on the forehead.

Gigi turned to Sofia, Antonio, and the house-keeper. "We must make sure she doesn't get an infection. We need to keep an eye on her."

Sofia and Antonio volunteered at the same time to watch her, but agreed it was unnecessary for both to be there together, so Sofia volunteered to come back later to relieve Antonio. Sofia and the housekeeper left, but Gigi stayed for a few more minutes.

Sarina started to feel the effects of the pain medication but still noticed the tender way Antonio caressed her cheek and the loving way he gazed at her.

"She will be okay, Antonio," Gigi said.

"I hope so," Antonio said without lifting his head.

Gigi nodded and slipped out of the room just as sleep overtook Sarina.

"My arm is on fire! My arm is on fire!" Sarina continued to scream as she ran around her bedroom with flames shooting from her arm. No one could hear her, so she stumbled out her bedroom door. She ran into Alfonso in the hallway.

"My arm is on fire!" she screamed.

"Serves you right for meddling in other people's affairs," Alfonso said. He walked away laughing.

She ran in the opposite direction and bumped into Aldo. Aldo reached out and squeezed her arm and Sarina let out a bloodcurdling scream.

"Sarina—Sarina, wake up."

Her eyes flew open and she tried to sit up but fell back against her pillow. She reached for her arm. "My arm."

Antonio reached out and held Sarina's left hand, caressed it. "It will be okay."

Her rapid heartbeat began to calm, and she tried to sit up again but fell back.

Antonio let go of Sarina's hand and wrapped his arms around her shoulders careful not to touch her right arm and lifted her into a sitting position. He didn't let go right away and he held Sarina close to him.

"This hurts like you would not believe," Sarina said.

"I can imagine," Antonio said. "But it isn't on fire anymore."

"What?" she asked.

"You were thrashing about and screaming that your arm was on fire," he said. "You were having a nightmare."

"Oh, I remember it now," Sarina said. "But it does feel like it is on fire."

"I can unwrap it and add more salve. That might help," Antonio said.

Sarina nodded and allowed Antonio to unwrap the bandages. They both gasped at the smell of rotten flesh and Sarina studied her swollen, bloody arm. Puss oozed in places.

"This looks like it is getting infected," Antonio said.

"Go get Gigi!"

Antonio started to give Sarina instructions on what to do until he came back when Sofia walked in the room. "Oh no! I am getting Gigi and calling the doctor."

The doctor's return trip to the villa didn't take long, and he inspected the wound first thing. He studied Sarina and said, "It appears she has a slight fever. I am going to give her some different medication and you need to administer it every six hours until the infection clears, and her fever subsides. If she is not showing any sign of improvement in a couple of days, you must call on me again."

Gigi and Antonio waited while Sofia walked the doctor out.

"I am not leaving until she is better," Antonio said.

"You have to rest and eat, Antonio. We are all here and able to help," Gigi said.

"I know, but I am not leaving," Antonio said. He walked across the room and sat next to Sarina and held her hand.

Gigi sighed and left the room.

Chapter Eighteen

Sarina flinched and looked around. Based on how dark it was outside she assumed it must be the middle of the night. She looked at her alarm clock and it read two in the morning. She started to adjust her position but stopped when she saw Nonna lean forward.

"Are you okay, dear?"

Sarina nodded. "Can I have a drink though?"

"Of course," Nonna reached over to the nightstand, picked up a cup of water and held it up to Sarina's mouth.

Sarina grabbed the cup. "I think I can do it."

Nonna let her take over. "You gave us quite a scare, Sarina. You had an infection from your burn that was fighting you hard. It was touch and go for a while. Gigi, Sofia, and I took turns caring for you, but Antonio never left your side. We went through regimens of caring for your wound and giving you medication. You would drift to sleep one minute and scream the next."

"I remember horrible nightmares of my arm being on fire and being chased by Aldo."

"I wondered if you were having nightmares based on some of your screams. We were scared for you and just when we thought we needed to take you to the hospital, your fever broke, the infection cleared, and you fell into a deep sleep."

"What day is it?" Sarina asked.

"It's Wednesday," Nonna said. "Well, actually based on the time it is early in the morning on Thursday."

She had missed two days. Sarina let that sink in while she glanced around the room. She noticed Antonio hunched in a bizarre position on the window seat. He looked to be sleeping. "How long has he been there?"

"He has been sleeping like that for a couple of hours."

Sarina looked at Nonna. "Will you wake him for me and tell him to come over here and lie down? That position can't be comfortable."

"I'm not sure I am comfortable with him sharing your bed," Nonna said.

"Well at least try and talk him into sleeping in a guest bedroom or something."

"We have tried that the past two nights, but he wouldn't budge."

Sarina felt her heart flutter as she gazed at Antonio. She wondered how much he must care for her to have stayed for so long. She evaluated her own feelings and found she cared for Antonio more than she probably should, especially since she still wasn't sure if she was going to stay or not.

She coughed, cleared her throat, and drank more water.

Antonio sat up, dropping a pillow he had been using, and looked over at Sarina. He crossed the room and kneeled on the side of the bed next to Nonna. He reached over and grabbed her hand. "Ah, my love. I am so happy to see you awake and much better."

Sarina squeezed his hand. "You have been so wonderful to watch over me, but please, Antonio, go get some rest."

"I can't leave you until I know you are going to be okay," he said.

"I am going to be fine," she encouraged. "Nonna will call you if there is a change. I promise. But that won't be necessary because I feel so much better. And the pain isn't as intense. Plus, my fever is gone."

Antonio appeared to study her. "I can refuse you nothing it seems. Fine, I will go rest in the guest room, but as soon as I wake up, I will return."

Sarina's heart soared and she grinned. "I look forward to it."

Antonio stood, kissed her, and walked out of the room.

"That boy is quite taken with you, Sarina," Nonna said as the door closed behind Antonio.

"I know," Sarina said. "I am quite taken with him too."

"And what will happen if you don't stay in Italy?" Nonna asked.

"Nonna I know what you are saying. I just—"

"You are just drawn to him," Sarina's grandmother finished for her. "Do you love him?"

Sarina considered her grandmother's question. "I'm not sure. Is it possible to love someone so quickly? I have never been in a relationship like this before. I have never loved anyone other than my parents, and I have never felt the way I do about Antonio. It scares me a little, you know?"

"Yes, I do know," her grandmother said. "Please be careful, Sarina. For both your sakes."

"I will, Nonna. I promise," Sarina tried to reassure.

Nonna smiled and patted Sarina's cheek. "Now let's clean up your arm, change the bandage, then you can get some more rest."

Sarina nodded and allowed her grandmother to clean the wound, reapply the salve, and wrap it back up. She closed her eyes and started to drift back to sleep but not before she heard Nonna whisper, "Oh, I fear for things to come."

When Sarina woke again, she found Antonio sitting in a chair by the bed with Sofia sitting on the opposite side on the edge of the bed.

"Hello," Sofia said as Sarina focused on her. Sarina sat up and Antonio leaned across the bed to kiss her on the cheek.

"You look so much better, Sarina," he said.

"How does your arm feel?" Sofia asked.

"Better than it did," Sarina said.

Sofia unwrapped the bandage, cleaned the burns, and reapplied the salve. Sofia started to rewrap the arm. "The doctor came by this morning while you were sleeping, and he said you shouldn't need skin grafts, but it was close. It was a bad burn and now that the infection is clearing up you should be okay. Nonna says you have to stay in bed one more day but if you are feeling better tomorrow you can get up."

Sarina grinned. "Can I at least take a shower?"

Antonio and Sofia laughed but shook their heads.

"That's probably not a good idea. But I can help you get into fresh pajamas and brush your hair," Sofia said.

Sarina sighed but agreed with her plan while Antonio left, saying he was going to get food for her.

When he returned, she was sitting up in bed wearing clean pajamas and Sofia was braiding her hair.

Antonio placed the tray of food on her lap, and she dove into the plate of cheese, bread, and grapes and washed it down with ice cold water.

"I was so hungry," Sarina said as Sofia finished braiding her hair.

Sarina finished eating and Antonio and Sofia picked apart the last few bits of food while they explained what happened when Sarina was out of it.

"The police and some firemen came out and did an investigation," Antonio said. "It was determined that the fire was set on purpose."

"They questioned Aldo and Marco," Sofia said. "But at this point no arrests have been made.

"Do they think they did it?" Sarina asked.

"Well, I think they are keeping that possibility open, but there is no proof right now and both have an alibi," Antonio explained. "They are following all leads as they come up."

Sarina nodded then changed the subject. "I know I have to lie in bed, but could I go lay outside on the balcony for a while and get some fresh air?"

Sofia and Antonio agreed fresh air might be good for the patient, so they helped cradle her arm and carry pillows to the chaise lounge. Once they knew Sarina was comfortable, Sofia cleaned the bathroom and took care of the dirty dishes, while Antonio put fresh sheets and blankets on her bed.

Sarina's eyes were closed when she heard Antonio come back outside. He kissed her on the forehead and whispered, "I will see you later, my love."

She was about to open her eyes but stopped when she heard Sofia say, "You love her."

"Is it that obvious?" he asked.

"It is to anyone who watches you with her," she said.

"I have never felt this way before, Sof," he said.

"Is she staying then?" Sofia asked.

"I don't know, and it scares me a little," Antonio said, "but I can't stop my heart from feeling this way. It just kind of happened. Before I knew it, I was— gone."

"Let's hope she stays then," Sofia said.

Sarina heard them leave and opened her eyes. She felt like her heart was pounding out of her chest as she looked out over the grounds.

What am I going to do?

She continued to look over the beautiful landscape contemplating what she had just heard until her eyes grew heavy, and she drifted off to sleep.

Sarina slept on and off for the rest of that day, and when the following day dawned, she felt better than she had all week. She got up on her own, took a shower, and dressed for the day. When she walked out of the bathroom, Gigi turned from the balcony door.

"Oh, there you are, my child," Gigi said. "How do you feel?"

"Much better," Sarina said.

"This is good," Gigi said. "Come, let's get your arm covered in medicine and wrapped, then you can come downstairs and join me for breakfast."

"That sounds wonderful," Sarina said. "I love this room but am ready to get out of it for a while."

Gigi laughed, put medication on her arm and wrapped it back up. She followed Gigi out of the room and down to the kitchen. They ate a light breakfast and Gigi explained how the cleanup was going. She thanked Sarina for all she had done to help put out the fire, even though she couldn't save the wine barrels.

"I am confused about something, though," Gigi said. "Why were there wine barrels in there at all? We usually don't store them in there."

"That is odd," Sarina said. "I was surprised too but thought maybe I misunderstood when I was learning things. I ran into the building to make sure there wasn't anything important in there because I honestly couldn't remember what it was used for."

"Your quick thinking saved my vineyard, Sarina," Gigi said.

"Oh ... I ... well ... I couldn't stand to see it burn," Sarina said. "It broke my heart to see it up in flames."

"Yes, which is why you should stay," Gigi said. "You have already developed a love for this place that some in the family have never had and never will. You are the rightful heir, but only you can decide to take it."

"I know, I just ..." Sarina trailed off.

"What is still holding you back?" Gigi asked.

Sarina thought about it. Her eyebrows furrowed and she frowned. "I don't know, just a feeling I have, I guess. Perhaps it's motivated by fear that if I make the wrong decision, I could ruin this place. Plus, there is a part of me that doesn't want to lose my farm at home."

"Who says you have to lose it. You could have a property management company take care of it for you," Gigi said.

"True," Sarina said. "It's all I have now of my past and I feel like if I let that go—"

"Then you let go of your father and his dreams, which is what you and your mother worked for?" Gigi finished.

"I feel like I am being torn between two worlds, two lives. One I didn't really want and felt lost in and one that I am falling in love with," Sarina explained. "But then there is the part that Mama and I worked so hard to continue my father's dream and could I really just let that go?"

"I don't want to pressure you, my dear," Gigi said. "Harvest is coming up in a week. But, if you are not ready to commit, perhaps we should give it more time. You can take as long as you need."

"Thank you for understanding," Sarina said. "I know my lack of decision is holding some people in limbo, but I can't help it. It's such a huge decision and I want to make sure it's the right one."

"Yes, you do have more time," Gigi said. "But consider all of the people here who will be hurt if you take a long time to decide, and in the end your decision is to leave."

Sarina knew her great-grandmother wasn't just talking about the family, but also Antonio. She didn't want to hurt anyone. Perhaps it was better if she pulled away from Antonio a little. She was afraid that starting a relationship without knowing her future was a mistake. It killed her to think of hurting him. Maybe it was better to stop things now, before they got too serious. Then if she did leave in the end, it wouldn't hurt as bad, for either of them. Sarina got up, kissed her great-grandmother on the cheek and walked toward the back door.

"Yes, sometimes a good walk helps ease the mind," Gigi said, "especially when it is as loaded as yours, my child."

"Thank you for understanding," Sarina said, and left the room.

Chapter Nineteen

I t had been two days since Sarina and her great-grandmother had the conversation in the kitchen about her future, and she didn't feel any closer to making a decision. The walk that day had only confused her more. The fire had ignited a love for the place that she hadn't realized she had.

She was feeling helpless when Sofia asked her if she wanted to go into town. Sofia was delivering wine and cheese to her brothers' restaurant again.

Sarina agreed and the two were off to the village.

"What is troubling you so?" Sofia asked her.

"I just wish I knew what to do," Sarina said.

"I think you should stay," Sofia said. "What does Iowa have for you, really? A house, some land? Land you told me you were probably going to end up selling, anyway."

"You make it sound so easy," Sarina said.

"Well maybe it is that easy," Sofia said.

"Antonio said the same thing," Sarina said, "I just ..."

"You're just scared," Sofia finished Sarina's thought.

"Yes—yes, I am scared," Sarina said. "I am afraid that if I stay and find out things about my mother that I'll wish I hadn't. I will want to flee that memory of her like she fled so many years ago. I am afraid that if I take over like Gigi says I should, that I will run this place into the ground. I am afraid that if I stay, and Antonio and I get serious, that he will decide to leave me once he really gets to know me. I am afraid that if I let go of Iowa that I will lose the only real memories I have of my parents."

Tears ran down her cheeks and she wanted to change the subject, but instead said, "I'm sorry, Sofia. I feel so lost again."

"First of all, stop apologizing all the time," Sofia said. "You don't ever have to apologize to me for being honest and speaking your mind. Second, you feel lost because you have not decided on a direction. I know that once you decide, you won't feel lost anymore. No matter what you decide, though, I will support you. I of course want you to stay but if you decide that the best thing for you is to leave then I will support you and come visit you as often as I can."

"Really?" Sarina asked. "You would come visit?"

"Of course, silly," Sofia said. "You and I have become good friends. Plus, we are family after all. And besides, who am I going to get excellent relationship advice from."

Sarina laughed. "How is Leone?"

"He is doing well. In fact, he wants us to go out with my parents and his parents. Kind of let them know how serious things are getting between the two of us."

"Sof, that is wonderful," she said. "I am so happy for you."

Sofia laughed. "Thank you. Again, I owe it to you."

"Not really, but I am happy to take the credit," Sarina said.

The subject changed to an even lighter tone as Sofia drove through town. The normal route was closed for street repairs, so she took a detour that went past Aldo's house. Sarina saw Aldo in his garden and Sarina asked her to stop.

"I'm not sure that is such a great idea, Sarina," Sofia said.

"Well, fate brought us here," Sarina said, so Sofia stopped the truck.

"Thank you," Sarina said as she hopped out. "Stay here though, okay?"

Sarina approached Aldo's gate and studied the man. He had a peace about him that she had not seen before, and she questioned if she'd misjudged him. But he must have heard her approaching because the peace changed when he looked over at her.

"What are you doing here?" Aldo asked. "Why won't you just leave me alone?" He turned and started walking toward his house.

"Wait please," Sarina pleaded. "I just want to talk to you. I am not my mother. Don't we all deserve to know the truth so that we can let this rest once and for all?"

Aldo paused and turned. She thought he was going to say something about her mother's case but instead he asked, "Why did you tell the police I burned your vineyard?"

Her eyes grew wide. "I didn't tell them that. In fact, I didn't even talk to them. But now that you brought it up, it makes sense, don't you think? You threaten me and a few days later my vineyard is up in flames."

"I didn't burn your vineyard. Now go," he snapped.

"How can I believe that?" she asked. "Just because you say you didn't? I don't believe you just like I don't believe that you are telling me everything about my mother and what happened."

Aldo's face changed again, and Sarina thought he looked as though a heavy weight was on his shoulders. "You do know what happened, don't you?"

Aldo acted as though he was going to say something but turned around and stomped into the house, slamming the door behind him.

Sarina tried to stop him. "Wait. Why won't you tell me?"

She sighed and her shoulders slumped forward as she walked back toward the truck and Sofia. She crawled in next to Sofia who said, "I'm sorry he wouldn't talk to you, but at least he wasn't as hostile as the last time. Maybe if you keep asking, he might give in and tell you."

Sarina nodded and Sofia drove on to her brothers' restaurant.

Sarina woke up the next day and remembered that she still had not spoken with her great-uncle. She hurried through getting ready for the day, grabbed her notes, and ran to her great-uncle's room. When she knocked on his door, she half expected not to get an answer so was surprised when she heard him say to enter.

Sarina opened the door and stuck her head in the room. "Uncle Tobia, I hope this is a good time, but I have needed to talk with you about a question I have on the ledgers."

Uncle Tobia motioned for her to come in and sit across from him. He was eating breakfast and she tried to apologize. He smiled. "It will be nice having a lovely companion while I eat." He offered her some food and she hesitated.

I am hungry. But she turned down the offer so she could discuss the ledgers and not get distracted.

"So, what seems be the trouble?" he asked.

"Well, I have been studying the books to get a better understanding of how things are run and where the vineyard and winery are financially," Sarina explained. "And perhaps even come up with ideas for the future. But then I noticed something in the ledger occasionally that concerns me."

Sarina pulled out the ledger and showed him the first tick mark. It was entered seven months prior to Sarina coming to Italy. She showed the same random tick mark every month in random places since that time. "I asked Gigi about it, but she wasn't sure what it meant. This concerned me a little, but I thought if you knew what it meant maybe I was just worrying over nothing."

Sarina's great-uncle stopped eating and grabbed the ledger. He studied it and said, "It appears there is something missing in the entry every time you see the tick mark."

"Right," Sarina said, "causing the books to not match at the end of that day. But the following day's entry shows the correct amount which then causes the ledger to even out again.

Sarina and Uncle Tobia pored over the ledgers and her notes pointing out different marks. She pointed at another mark and asked, "Do you think there is another ledger book somewhere?"

"I would say so," he said. "I don't like how this looks, Sarina."

"I don't either, Uncle Tobia," Sarina said. "I don't want to blame anyone for anything yet, but do you think someone is stealing from the vineyard?"

"It appears that way," he agreed.

"Who do you think it is?" she asked. She had come to her own conclusion, but she didn't want to say anything.

"You know who it is, same as I do," he said. "And I must say this does not surprise me. He always felt like he should be the heir because he did so much for this place, but when it looked like that would never be a reality, he became bitter. He threatened to leave awhile back, but he never did. This must be why. He must have decided to steal from the vineyard first. Mother is going to be heartbroken."

"Do you think she suspects?" Sarina asked.

"She probably does," Uncle Tobia said. "She misses very little."

"Well, I guess the next thing I need to do is try to find that missing ledger," Sarina said.

"I agree," he said. "I would look in his private office in the loft of the wine barn. If it isn't there, I would look in his room. Chances are, though, he is keeping it in his office under lock and key, so you might have to break into it."

"That is what I was afraid of," she said.

"I suppose it goes without saying that you can't let anyone see you or know what you are doing until we have the ledger and find out for sure," he explained.

"I agree," Sarina said. "I will be careful."

"Thank you for bringing this to me, Sarina," Uncle Tobia said. "Mother was right. You do love this place and want the best for it. It is hard to stand against family when they are wrong but someone with strength like you is what is needed here."

"There are others here who have strength," she said.

"Perhaps, but you are special," he said, "Plus, you are the first born, of a first born, and as such, the rightful heir."

Sarina smiled, thanked her great-uncle, and said they should talk more often. He agreed. She gathered the ledgers and her notes and went back to her room. She tucked everything away for later and went in search of her own breakfast.

Sarina was finishing the scones and grapes she'd found to eat when Antonio walked into the kitchen.

"There you are, Sarina," he said. "I have been look-ing for you."

Sarina smiled and her heart skipped a beat as it always did when he turned his smile on her. Her smiled faltered when she remembered the conversation she needed to have with him.

"What is it?" he asked.

"I just ..." Sarina trailed off. She took a deep breath and said, "We need to talk."

He frowned and sat next to her. "I guess I am not surprised since you have been distant and all but avoiding me the past couple of days."

"Antonio," she started. "You know I care for you."

"Stop, Sarina," Antonio said. "If you are about to break things off, just tell me. Don't give me a speech about how you care for me."

The hurt in his eyes went straight through Sarina's heart. She reached out to take his hand, but Antonio stood.

He started pacing. "Are you leaving?"

"No, well—I don't know, Antonio," Sarina said. "And until I know what my future is, how I can pretend to build one with you?"

"So, this has all been pretend for you?" he asked.

"No. Not at all," Sarina said. "You have to know that I care for you."

"Yes, well I love you, Sarina!" Antonio shouted. He threw up his hands as though he were frustrated or hurt and said, "You know I was prepared to make things work no matter your decision, but you come in here and hurt me. You will hurt Gigi. You will hurt Sofia, and you will hurt the rest of your family. The longer you are here the more your family wants you to stay. The more I want you to stay. If you are going to leave, you need to just do it and spare us all the pain and heartache."

Sarina stood and started across the room to Antonio, to the man she realized she loved. Her heart shattered and she regretted ever allowing this.

He took a step back and he held up his hand. "Don't, just don't, Sarina. Once you make up your mind, let me know!" Antonio stormed past her out the back door and slammed the door behind him.

She watched him leave. *What have I done? What am I doing here? Why is this all so damn complicated?* Sarina whirled around and ran up to her bedroom. She fell on her bed and let her tears pour out.

She wallowed in her sorrow and heartache while her mind raced. She thought about all that had happened since she arrived. She thought about Iowa and her mother and gasped. She remembered the keepsake box. Wanting to feel close to her mother, she retrieved it from its hiding place in the armoire, and sat with it in front of the balcony.

Sarina pulled out the locket that always rested around her neck and opened the secret compartment to reveal the hidden key. She unlocked the keepsake box, stashed the key back into its hiding place, and lifted the lid.

The picture of her mother and father standing on the hill overlooking the town and sea was the first thing she saw. Sarina remembered that spot from the day she arrived. That seemed so long ago now. She set the picture aside and sifted through the box. One letter caught her eye, so she lifted it out. It was one her mother had written to her grandmother but had never sent.

> My dearest mother,
>
> It has been so long since I have seen you last. The cancer is taking its toll on me now and I often wonder if I will survive this. My Sarina has been a huge help to me, but I can't help but feel she is lost here. Her father and I had wanted to create a safe place and a future for her here. I always knew I could never take her to Italy but now I wonder if I have taken her future from her by not taking her.
>
> She acts like she is content working in the little accounting office in town and then coming home to care for me and doing school at night, but I know

she wants more. And I wanted so much more for her. I think I have crippled her. I have decided that I must send her to you upon my passing. My hope is that she will finally find a place where she no longer feels lost or confused about her purpose.

She reminds me of myself when I was young, but she has the wisdom of Gigi about her. It amazes me how much she looks just like Gigi. I don't think I have ever told her that. But talking of home was too painful for so long and now it's just a habit to not discuss it, I think. Sarina will be home soon, and I grow tired. Tired of it all, my only thought anymore is what will happen of my Sarina after I am gone.

The letter stopped and Sarina could only assume that either she had come home, or the nurse had interrupted her. Or Mama had simply just fallen asleep. Sarina read the letter a second time and wondered at the concern her mother had for her. Sarina realized no matter how much she'd tried to mask her discontent in her life, her mother had seen right through her.

Sarina looked back in the box and saw the letter her mother had written for her. The same one that Sarina had read right after her passing and she pulled it out and reread it. One part seemed to jump off the page at her.

"I fully believe that your promise to me will lead you to where you are meant to go. It will take you on the journey that is meant for you. Your destiny. Your fate. Your calling. You have so much to offer in this life, my sweet girl, and you can no longer stay in our tiny little house in our tiny little town. This is your time. Take it! Take it without fear, even when at times it is scary."

Sarina realized what she had to do and what she was meant to do. She was to stay. A huge weight lifted off her shoulders and she thought of Antonio. What had she done? Sarina threw the letters and pictures aside and ran out of her room in search of her love.

Sarina got to the living room when she heard the housekeeper answer a ringing phone.

"Sarina, it is for you," she said.

"Take a message," Sarina said.

"He says it's urgent," the housekeeper said. "It's Marco."

"Marco?" Sarina said and decided to take the call.

"Hello," she said.

"Sarina?" Marco asked.

"Yes," she said. "I know it's you, Marco. What do you want?"

"I must talk with you, right away," Marco said. "Meet me at the village graveyard next to Bernado's grave in twenty minutes."

The line went dead.

Sarina stared at the phone, wondering what this could mean. She placed the phone in its cradle, grabbed Sofia's truck keys, and left.

Chapter Twenty

Sarina parked the truck alongside a row of graves when she saw Marco. He was standing next to a gravestone she assumed was Bernado's. She wasn't sure if this was such a good idea, but knew he had answers and she was ready to risk it all for them. She climbed out of the truck and crossed to Marco and stopped a few feet short of him.

Sarina could hear the occasional bird or gust of wind, but otherwise the silence was deafening. She went to step closer when Marco started talking.

"He was my best friend, you know," Marco explained. "I had no one, really. My own mother died when I was a child, and my father was a fisherman and was gone all the time, so I was often left to tend to myself. Bernado took pity on me and I stayed at his place most of the time as we got older. We were like brothers. Aldo was like a father to me too and still is."

Sarina took a cautious step closer this time but didn't say anything for fear Marco would stop talking.

"Bernado had a thing for your mama," Marco continued. "I think she knew it too, but she was with Stefano, so that was never going to happen. The night of the festival was a crazy night. Bernado and me, well, we were supposed to go to the festival with a couple of girls from the next town but when they arrived at the festival, they decided they had better odds of meeting up with better men. At least that is what they told Bernado."

He paused ran his fingers through his hair. "He was pretty hurt and mad about it, so he started drinking. I joined in drinking a little but he didn't stop. I don't think I ever saw him drink that much. At one point I told him we should just head on home and have him sleep it off. Bernado agreed at first, but then he saw your mama and Stefano arguing and your mama stomp off.

Marco looked at Sarina and back to his friend's grave. "He told me maybe it was time to show that girl what a real man was and followed her. I followed along, trying to change his mind, but there was no changing it."

Sarina could feel unease at how the story was going and sat on a bench next to Marco.

"Your mama was walking pretty fast," Marco continued. "But at one point she dropped a scarf she was wearing on the ground. As she bent to pick it up, we caught up to her. She must have heard us because she seemed startled at first, but then she saw it was us and laughed a little, saying that we had scared her."

Marco sat next to Sarina. "Bernado said there was no reason to be scared of him and he started walking closer to her. I could tell she smelled the liquor on this breath, and it seemed to make her nervous, so she said, 'Well have a good evening,' and turned and started to walk away, leaving the scarf on the ground. I actually stopped and picked it up."

He went quiet for a moment then pulled a dainty pale pink scarf from his pocket and stared at it.

Sarina froze. *I knew it. He was there and the scarf is proof.*

"Bernado started to stumble after her," Marco continued, "and when he was struggling to stay on his feet he hollered for me to catch her. I knew we were being reckless, but my loyalty to Bernado won out and I went after her and grabbed her arm. Your mama put up a fight. She tried to pull away and in that struggle, the sleeve of her dress tore. She looked at me with fear in her eyes and I let her go. But by that point Bernado had caught up to us and grabbed her. But in his haste and imbalance, the two fell over and onto the ground. Your mama hit her head hard on the curb."

Sarina shifted away from Marco so she could look at him. She placed her hand on her pounding heart.

Marco turned to look at Bernado's grave and said, "She made this moaning sound, and her eyes were closed. Well, this seemed to ignite a fire in Bernado, one which I had not seen before. He decided he was going to take her right then." Marco started moving his arms like he was acting out the motions. "He ripped open the front of her dress without resistance, but he was rough when he tore it and that seemed to wake her up a little. She started to struggle against him which only seemed to excite him more."

"At one point she looked over at me and said, 'Help me, please.'" Marco paused and looked at Sarina. "I didn't know what to do. I started to walk over to them, but he pulled out a knife and told me to stay back or he was going to kill me, then her. It was his father's hunting knife. He had taken it for some reason and to this day I am not sure what that reason was."

"When I saw the knife," Marco continued, "I froze. I was shocked by how he was acting. It had to mostly be the alcohol, but I think years of frustration of not being able to get close to your mama, and years of frustration of having a tough father all came to a head that night. When Bernado was focused on me, your mama was able to wiggle a little and started to get free from his grasp. And since he was so clumsy and drunk, she was able to get away from him for just a minute. He got up and tried to tackle her, but missed and in the last second snagged the bottom of her dress which ripped. She stumbled and fell to the ground momentarily, but jumped up again and tried to run."

Marco stared at the scarf once more. "Bernado thought he was too fast for her, despite being drunk, and he lunged for her again. This time he tackled her, knocking her to the ground again, and it caused her to hit her head a second time. The force of the lunge made them roll and when they finally stopped, Bernado lay motionless on top of your mama and your mama was out cold.

"I checked Bernado and when I saw the blood, I knew he was dead. The knife lay a few inches from him and I knew he must have fallen and rolled on his knife. I panicked and took off running. I ran all the way to Aldo's and stayed there until he came home. I didn't tell him what happened, and I let him and the rest of the town, come to their own conclusions."

Sarina trembled, her heart thundered in her chest and she felt a rage wash over her when she stammered, "How could you? What purpose did you have in keeping it a secret?"

"I had to protect him," Marco tried to explain. "I couldn't let his last act for all to see be of him attacking and trying to rape a woman."

"So, you let my precious Mama be the one to bear the brunt of all the resentment and anger and lies," Sarina said.

"I was sorry for that," Marco said. "But I couldn't say anything after things became such a huge mess. I would have gone to jail and I just couldn't handle that."

Sarina stood and walked toward Bernado's grave. She looked at it and felt empty. She felt cold. She felt anger. Sarina turned toward Marco. "You caused an innocent woman to break up a happy relationship and flee town and her family and never return. You let an innocent woman live her entire life with a guilt and heartache that could never be eased because she couldn't remember what happened and thought the worst of herself. What kind of monster are you to do that to another human being? You chose the side of a rapist!" Sarina realized she was yelling.

Marco only stared at her in response.

"It's no use talking to you further, is it?" Sarina asked, turned, and started to walk away. "I am going straight to the police and if I were you, I would get a really good lawyer."

"I can't let you do that," Marco said.

"Watch me," she said, but paused when she heard an unfamiliar sound. It sent a tingle up her spine and warning bells went off in her mind as she cautiously turned back around. Marco held a pistol, and it was aimed at her. Sarina put her arms up and started to back away.

"Stop! Just stop!" Marco screamed. "Why did you have to come here and ruin everything? This was all in the past where it belonged, and you had to come here and stir things up!"

"It would never have been left in the past, Marco, and you know it," Sarina said. "The truth would have eventually eaten you alive, which is evident by the way you are acting now."

"Stop talking!" Marco screamed and his hand began to tremble.

Am I going to make it out of here alive?

Marco's expression changed to what looked like alarm and he asked, "What are you doing here?"

Sarina was sure she looked confused, but she understood soon when a voice behind her said, "I heard you on the phone and I decided it might be best for me to come and see what you were doing."

Sarina's heart sank when she turned to see who was talking. It was Aldo. She knew she would never be able to get out of there.

"How long have you been here?" Marco asked Aldo.

"Long enough," Aldo said.

Aldo sounded tired and resigned, as though he were giving in to something. He walked closer to Marco. "Put the gun down, son."

Sarina was stunned, but took a step back.

"What?" Marco asked. "How can you say that? This girl needs to be gone so our lives can go back to the way they were."

"Really, Marco?" Aldo asked. "You want to grow more and more suspicious of people, apparently fearing that they found you out? Letting me wallow in the heartache of losing my son and wondering the truth of what really happened, fearing he had done something horrible and growing more bitter from it with each passing day."

Marco shook all over and tears rained down his cheeks. "I can't let this continue."

"It's over, Marco," Aldo said.

He might shoot both of us.

Marco looked from Aldo to Sarina, and back at Aldo. "I did this for you, you know," Marco said. "And for Bernado. But I see it was for nothing."

Marco turned the gun toward his own head and pulled the trigger.

Sarina and Aldo screamed at the same time and Marco fell to the ground, a pool of blood seeping out around his head.

Sarina heard bloodcurdling screams, and it took her a minute to realize they were her own. Her body trembled violently, and she couldn't stop the sobs that racked her body. She was hysterical when Aldo reached out to her. She flinched, stumbled backwards, covered her face with her hands, and collapsed to the ground.

"I'm so sorry, Sarina," Aldo cried. "I don't know what to say."

She sat in a crumpled heap until she was able to force herself to gain some semblance of composure.

"I'm—um—I'm sorry too," Sarina said in between hiccups. "I thought you knew what happened."

"I had an idea but didn't know for sure," Aldo explained. "I knew Bernado must have been provoking a fight or something when I saw the knife. It was my knife after all, but all I could think about at the time was protecting my son and protecting the only family I had left."

"Marco," Sarina whispered.

"Yes, Marco." Aldo brushed tears away while he stared at the dead body of the man that had been like a son to him for so many years. He turned to Sarina. "You should go."

"Shouldn't I stay, after all, we need to talk to the police, let them know what happened," Sarina said. When Aldo didn't say anything at first, Sarina started to shake with anger this time. "I hope you're not expecting me to keep quiet or allow you to brush this all under the rug again."

Aldo sighed and looked at her with what seemed to be anguish. "No, Sarina. I will tell the police everything. You have my word. I swear on your mother's grave that I will take care of this."

Sarina decided she could trust him and stumbled to the truck. When she got there, she stopped and looked at Aldo. He was kneeling over Marco, his body shaking with sobs. She felt a wave of emotions rush through her, and she fought back the dam of tears. *Such pain must have lived in his heart for as long as it lived Mama's.* She hoped he could at least find some peace now. She turned, crawled into the truck, and drove away.

So many feelings hammered through her when she arrived back at the villa. She was glad she could share what happened to her mama with the rest of her family. Plus, she was happy she would be able to tell them she was going to stay. But she was also still wrecked and in shock over what happened to Marco.

Sarina pulled into a spot to park and found so many cars parked along the side of the house. She realized that a family meeting must have been called. She felt a surge of guilt for not being there but believed she would be forgiven once she explained why she was late.

Voices were raised in the great room, so Sarina knew to head there. But when the housekeeper saw her, she gave Sarina a strange look and Sarina felt sick to her stomach. She neared the foyer when she realized the voices were amid a heated conversation, but she continued until she heard her name.

Sarina stopped. It was her cousin Cosimo the third's voice she heard, "I really think the evidence points to Sarina. She is a stranger after all. Besides, I overheard a conversation about the ledgers, and she has been closed mouth about it. I think she may be trying to steal from us. Maybe even ruin us so that she can cut her loses, take what money she can, and go back to America. I mean isn't that why she hasn't committed to staying after all?"

"That is absurd," Sofia said.

"She is an American after all. And we all know Americans are greedy."

Several people started yelling at the same time, and they all agreed with Cosimo. A few defended Sarina, but the loudest voices were accusing her of stealing from the winery and burning the vineyard. She felt the pain in her heart grow. Sarina tried to smile when she heard someone else remind the family that she'd been hurt during the fire. But Alfonso said, "What a perfect cover. Get hurt to throw off suspicion. And let's not forget she knew the barrels were in there. How could she have known unless she placed them in there herself?"

When Sarina didn't hear anyone else defend her after Alfonso's speech, she had heard enough. She turned back toward the kitchen and ran out into the courtyard. Sarina decided she had to clear her name. Then, she would have to leave.

She realized she was going to flee Italy in pain, just as her mother had done.

Sarina felt pain, but she also felt an anger toward her mother for sending her to Italy at all. The anger continued to build in her, along with the other emotions of the day, while she walked into the wine barn. She found her way up to the loft where Alfonso's office was. Her great-uncle was right, the door was locked, and Sarina looked around for a way to break into it. She found a crowbar and with her anger, determination, and hurt, she was able to bust open the lock with little effort.

She hurried over to a large desk and started to look for the proof of her innocence. She shuffled through a few drawers and items on top of the desk, but found nothing. She refused to give up and continued to fumble through everything and noticed a small lever. She pushed it and it opened a secret drawer with a lid. Sarina tried to open it but found it was locked. Sarina grabbed the crowbar and slammed it against the drawer. The lid popped open.

Sarina looked inside and nestled in its confines was a small notebook. She picked it up and thumbed through it. Here was the proof she needed. Sarina studied the notebook long enough to make sure this was all she needed and realized her cousin had stolen almost a half a million dollars so far. When she thumbed through to the last entry, a document fell out. Sarina bent down, picked it up and gasped when she opened it.

The document was a contract to sell off the bulk of the estate, including the villa with intentions of turning it into a resort. Sarina stuffed the contract back into the notebook, shut the drawer and left the office. Sarina didn't bother with covering her tracks because by the time her cousin saw the broken lock she would be long gone. And the contents of the broken drawer would be in her great-grandmother's hands.

Sarina rushed back to the house and snuck up to her room. Tears stung her eyes as she started to pack. She had to take a break and catch her breath after a few minutes, so she sat on her bed and looked around. *I could have been happy here, but there is no way that is possible now.* Sarina tried to stop shaking when she picked up the phone and called the airline, then a car to run her to the airport.

She finished packing and decided to write letters to her grandmother and great-grandmother to explain everything. She wrote that she hoped the family would find peace at last. Sarina decided to leave her mother's ashes and explained that in the letters as well.

At the end of the letters, Sarina said how much she loved them all and would miss them. And she thanked them for everything they had done for her. She signed both letters—I will forever hold you in my heart— gathered the letters and all the evidence, minus the ledgers, and placed them in the keepsake box. She grabbed the tiny key out of its hiding place in her locket, stuffed it in an envelope and taped it to the top of the keepsake box.

About an hour after Sarina finished her preparations, there was a knock on her door and her great-grandmother peeked her head around the door. *She looks weary, or maybe it's the shadows of the darkened room.*

Gigi had a look of surprise on her face when she saw Sarina was already in bed. "Are you okay?"

"Just tired," Sarina said, "and my arm hurts so I thought I would go to bed early."

"You should come join me for dinner," Gigi offered.

"Actually," Sarina said, "I am not really hungry. I think I will sleep for now."

"Okay. I was hoping to talk with you, but it can wait," Gigi crossed the room, kissed Sarina on the forehead and left.

Maybe I am jumping to conclusions. Maybe I am acting hasty. But the memory of the accusations and hateful words rushed back along with the shock and emotions of what happened with Marco, so Sarina resolved to leave early in the morning. She drifted off into a restless night of sleep.

Chapter Twenty-One

S arina looked out the window of the plane as it started to taxi on the runway. She decided to fly back to Iowa first class again, for her heart hurt too much to deal with cramped quarters. She was sipping an ice-cold cocktail and her eyes grew misty as the ground started to get smaller and smaller. She thought she knew pain when her mother died, but this was worse. Almost.

What am I even going back to? To a home that is really an empty house and to farmland I don't know what to do with? Maybe I could create my own vineyard. No, all I would think about is them and the villa. Sarina shifted in her seat, and tried to think of something, anything, but the Giacoletti's.

Antonio!

As soon as his name sprang to mind, Sarina tried to brush it aside. But her thoughts persisted. *What would he say?* She had left him a note along with those for her great-grandmother and grandmother. Sarina fidgeted in her seat, messed with the collar of her shirt, took another sip of her cocktail. *And what about*

Sofia? Sarina thought about the cousin who had become a friend, almost like a sister, and brushed away a tear.

Sarina had borrowed Sofia's truck early that morning, drove it into town, and parked it behind her cousins' restaurant. She left a note for Sofia which said she was sorry that she was leaving this way, but she couldn't handle the family thinking she'd burned the vineyard and would try to steal from them. She shifted in her seat again and prayed that Sofia would forgive her. *I hope she keeps her promise one day and comes to Neely.*

She drained the rest of her cocktail, handed it to the flight attendant walking by, and closed her eyes. Sarina tried to sleep but couldn't stop thinking about what to do with her home in Neely, and whether she would ever find peace, belonging, and love again.

Gigi sat up, rubbed her eyes, looked around her room, and thought about the family meeting the night before. She knew Sarina was innocent, as did most of the family, but the few who were pointing fingers were so convincing, she could tell some were beginning to waver. She requested the family gather proof of what they were saying and get back with her.

I need to face this head on. She threw back her covers and prepared to face the day. It didn't take long for her to get dressed and she decided to get breakfast before meeting with Sarina. Gigi started to leave her room but stopped when she noticed the keepsake box with an envelope on top. It was tucked out of the way, so she hadn't noticed it before now.

It was the keepsake box she had given to Luc all those years ago. Gigi leaned down to pick it up and noticed the ledgers next to it. She stacked them on top of the box and carried them over to her desk. She peeked inside the envelope, saw the key, and used it to open the keepsake box. Inside were pictures and letters, but what caught her attention were the two envelopes on top and a small notebook.

Gigi lifted the notebook. She was concerned the information might implicate Sarina, but soon realized this was from her and it was proof of her innocence. Gigi moved on to the letter addressed to her, and she couldn't read it fast enough. Her hands shook with each passing sentence.

"No!" Gigi dropped the letter and rushed to Sarina's room.

She entered Sarina's bedroom and found it dark and empty. She cried out again. Gigi rushed through the room looking for any sign that her fear was not warranted but found Sarina was gone and so were her things.

"What have we done?" Gigi gasped. Gigi rushed out of Sarina's room back to her own room and with a trembling hand, picked up her phone. She dialed the number and heard a voice answer.

"She's gone."

Gigi called the family together, so everyone was gathered in the same living room as they had been the day before. The few people who knew what had occurred had not shared it with anyone else because Gigi wanted to share it with everyone together. She had given Giada her letter and she had expressed how much her heart was broken and how they had failed to honor Luc's memory by allowing Sarina's fate to be much the same as Luc's. Fleeing Italy in pain.

Sofia was making a comment to her brother that she noticed her pickup was gone, and it brought Gigi back to the present.

"I don't know where it is," Sofia said as Gigi cleared her throat.

The room that had once been a bustle of activity and voices, stilled instantly upon seeing Gigi's ashen face. Gigi noticed Sofia look around the room like she was looking for someone and when she caught Giada's eye she mouthed, "Where is Sarina?"

Giada made a motion with her head as though to say focus on Gigi.

"First, I would like to share some information regarding the fire," Gigi said. "There has been some new evidence brought to light."

Gigi stood in front of a small table with the ledgers, the small notebook, Alfonso's contract, and her letter from Sarina stacked in front of her. She picked up the contract and noticed Alfonso go pale and squirm in his seat.

"Someone in the family is stealing money from the vineyard," she said. "And there is proof on which family member it is. There is also circumstantial evidence that this family member set the fire as well."

Alfonso stood. "I don't have time for this, I have work to do."

Gigi shouted for Tito to stop him. Tito complied and forced Alfonso to sit. Gigi walked over to Alfonso. "I have never in my life felt so betrayed by anyone in the family."

She started to shake. "You have stolen from your family and its legacy and in the process hurt the family. You also tried to burn the vineyard in hopes that I would sell it to some businessmen. What do you have to say for yourself?"

Alfonso stared at his hands and stayed quiet.

"Well, I obviously had more faith in your abilities than I should have given you credit for," Gigi said, "because this scheme of yours would never have worked. And the fact that you did not realize that, well it just goes to show how much you don't understand this place and what it stands for."

Gigi paused and took a deep breath. "You are no longer a part of this family, Alfonso. The police have been called and they will be here soon."

Everyone started to talk at the same time. Those who had accused Sarina changed their stories. Cosimo the third was beet red. Anna picked at her dress and stuck out her chin as though to say I was only supporting my son.

Gigi turned from Alfonso, who sat motionless, while Tito stood guard over him, and walked back to the table. She picked up the letter from Sarina and wiped at her face. She glanced at Antonio who was sitting in the corner. He seemed confused as though he wasn't sure why he was called to the family meeting. He looked over at Giada and she smiled sadly at him.

"I have something else to share," Gigi said. "The mystery around the incident involving our Luciana has been solved. When the police arrive, they will back up what I am about to say, but Sarina was able to find out the truth.

"Where is Sarina?" Antonio asked.

Gigi looked at him. "I'm getting to that, but first I want to share what happened to Luciana."

She unfolded the letter from Sarina and read the part explaining the details of her meeting with Marco and Aldo and how Marco shot himself in front of her.

The whole family erupted once more. They asked questions, some were crying, and Antonio walked to the middle of the room.

"Where is Sarina?" he shouted.

The room fell silent at Antonio's outburst. And all Gigi could do was shake her head while tears ran down her cheeks.

"No!" Antonio shouted and ran out of the room.

Sofia walked forward. "What is going on? Where is she?"

Gigi felt her heart shatter. "She left."

Sofia made a gasping sound and asked, "Why?"

"She left because she felt betrayed by all of us," Gigi explained. "She heard the meeting yesterday and the accusations—unfounded accusations—against her. We forced her to leave much the same way her mother left. She felt like she had to flee because she was hurt—by all of us."

Gigi paused and looked around the room. "I have never been as ashamed of my family as I am now. We lost our Luciana long ago and she gave us her daughter for safe keeping. We betrayed them both." Gigi felt defeated and leaned against the table.

Several members of the family stood ashen faced with tears in their eyes; others were talking and arguing amongst themselves about who was more to blame. Giada was crying and being comforted by Cosimo. Sofia ran out of the room. Gigi followed Sofia calling for her to come back.

Gigi had tears streaming down her face when she finally reached Sofia, who was stopped inside Sarina's bedroom doorway. She peered around Sofia to see what stopped her and found Antonio kneeling in the center of the room with his face in his hands. Gigi knew the moment he realized they were there, because he looked in their direction and took a deep breath.

"We have to go get her."

Sarina walked through the sliding doors of the airport and felt the rush of humid air. It was supposed to be fall, but there appeared to be a few more humid days left. She looked around and saw the truck coming toward her with Todd in the driver's seat. She waved at the young man as he stopped by the curb and jumped out.

"Welcome home," Todd said. He came around the side of the truck and loaded her luggage.

"Thanks," Sarina said.

She climbed into the cab, felt the gush of the AC, and sighed. It felt good in contrast to the humid air outside. Todd climbed in and glanced her way, buckled himself in, and drove off. Sarina wondered if he could see how sad she felt.

Todd attempted to ask a few questions about Italy, but Sarina was dismissive in her answers. She was relieved that he got the hint and stopped talking to her. They rode the rest of the way to her house in silence.

She stared out at the countryside and realized she had not missed it. She wished she was back home in Vetualini. *Funny, I never thought of Vetualini as home, until now. Home, where is home going to be for me now.* Sarina thought it was going to be in Neely, but now she wasn't sure. The villa had been more of a home to her in the last month than Neely ever was.

Todd pulled into the driveway of Sarina's house and she was thankful that at least the journey back to Neely was complete. Her shoulders slumped forward, and she frowned. *So much has happened and all I want now is my bed and some sleep.*

Sarina opened her door and climbed out of the truck. She set her shoulders as though to brace for the humidity that took her breath away.

She walked the few feet to the front porch and climbed the stairs. Mary burst out the front door and pulled her into a hug. Sarina hadn't realized how much she needed to be held until this moment and burst into tears.

"Oh, Sarina. What's wrong?" Mary asked.

Sarina didn't respond, so Mary led her into the house while Todd unloaded the truck.

They sat at the kitchen table and Sarina looked around the room. It seemed so foreign to her now.

Mary put a large glass of lemonade into Sarina's hands. "Drink that, dear. It will do you good on such a hot day and after such a long trip."

Sarina stared at her glass, took a drink, and said, "It was so hard to leave there and come back."

"Then why did you?" Mary asked.

"It's a long story," Sarina said.

"Well, I have all afternoon if you want to share," Mary said.

"Let's just say that the family was wonderful at first and a few of them were really genuine," she said. But in the end they were not as wonderful and genuinely hated me."

"I doubt they hated you, Sarina," Mary said. "What happened for you to think that?"

"Long story short, there was a fire, and they think I set it," Sarina said.

"What happened to your arm?" Mary asked.

"I was trying to put out the fire and got burned," Sarina explained.

"Oh no, Sarina. Are you okay?" Mary asked.

"The burn is healing well," Sarina said.

"Perhaps there was a misunderstanding, and they are upset you left?" Mary asked.

"I doubt it," Sarina said.

Sarina yawned, brushed at her eyes that were wet with tears, and stood. "All I want to do now is sleep."

"I think that is a good idea," Mary said. "You go rest. I will tidy up here and let myself out. And later, when you need to talk more, I will be here."

Sarina smiled at her neighbor and left the room.

Sarina woke and looked around the room. It took her a minute to remember she was back in Neely. She sighed and heard her stomach growl. She threw her covers to the side and went down to the kitchen to find something to eat.

She opened her refrigerator and realized Mary had stocked it for her. She smiled at her neighbor's kindness. "Bless you, Mary," Sarina mumbled and made a ham and cheese sandwich. She felt a pang when she compared the cheese to what she had been eating while at the villa.

Sarina tried to push thoughts of Italy away as she placed her plate on the kitchen table. She retrieved a glass of lemonade and sat to eat. The room took on an eerie feeling with each bite, and she realized it was because it was so quiet.

Gone was the hustle and bustle and constant noise and voices of the villa. Once again, Sarina longed for it. She felt a lump in the back of her throat. She knew if she couldn't stop thinking about Italy, her emotions would take over, and she just didn't want to deal with that right now.

Sarina forced thoughts of Italy aside once more, looked around her kitchen and wondered what she was going to do with the place. There was a time growing up when she loved it here, but not anymore. This place no longer felt like home. She got up from the kitchen table with sandwich in hand, walked around the first floor of the house, and contemplated what she was going to do now.

I can't go back to Italy, especially after the way I left. And I can't stay here. This place is no longer home. The trip to Italy made her realize she truly didn't belong here, and it was time to go. Sarina decided to go into town in the morning and buy a for sale sign.

Chapter Twenty-Two

Sarina had only one thought in mind as she pedaled into town—stop thinking about Vetualini. Thoughts of Vetualini were difficult to bear. She decided if she got away from Neely, all ties and painful memories to the past would be left behind. She realized that she could take her precious memories anywhere and didn't need to keep the farm.

She crested the hill where she always liked to stop. She remembered the last time she had ridden her bike into town—it was the day her mother died. Sarina stopped her bike and studied the road that led out of town—*not too much longer and I will be gone*—Sarina smiled and pedaled on.

The hardware store hummed with the sounds of business as Sarina walked up and down the aisles. She was looking for a specific sign. She found what she needed and walked to the counter to pay. It seemed strange to be able to hear people's conversations and understand them. Her family always spoke in English with her, but when they were in town or around other people, all she'd heard was Italian.

Stop it, you have to stop thinking about Vetualini, the villa, the family, all of it.

Thoughts of Antonio blasted into her mind and she winced. Her knees became weak and she had to lean on the counter to keep from falling.

"Um, you okay, Sarina?" the store clerk asked.

"Yes," she said. "Just tired I guess."

"Hey that's right, you just got back from Italy," the store clerk said. "How was it?"

"It was fine," Sarina mumbled.

"Well, welcome home," the store clerk said.

"Thanks," she said, paid for her items and left the store.

Sarina tied everything to her bike and rode back toward her house. As she rounded the corner where she had worked at the accountant's office, her old boss, Frank, came out and waved at her to flag her down.

She stopped and tried to smile.

"So, Sarina you're back now?" Frank asked. "When can I expect you on the books again?"

Sarina cleared her throat. "Actually, Frank, I won't be returning. I have decided to sell the farm and relocate somewhere else."

"Somewhere else?" Frank asked. "Italy?"

"I'm not sure yet," she said. "But once I decide I will be gone."

Frank scratched his head. "I see. I must say I'm not surprised. I knew this day would come eventually. You are destined for more. Well, if you need a reference, let me know."

"Thank you, Frank," she said. She waved at her old boss and rode away.

Fifteen minutes later she pulled into her driveway. She saw Mary sitting on her front porch. The two women waved at each other as Sarina parked her bike. Sarina unfastened the items she bought in town and asked Mary if she would help her a minute.

"Of course," Mary said and followed Sarina toward the end of the driveway.

"Can you hold this in place for me?" Sarina asked.

"Um, sure," Mary said and held the sign steady.

Sarina hammered the sign into the ground, nodded and said, "Well, that's done then."

Sarina and Mary took a few steps back to inspect their handiwork. Mary gasped and they looked at each other as Mary asked, "You can't really mean to sell the place?"

I have to," Sarina said. "I don't belong here."

"But where will you go?" Mary asked.

"I haven't figured that out yet," Sarina said. "I was thinking maybe California or Texas or the east coast. I'm really not sure. Wherever I go has to have some land though as I think I want to start a vineyard or winery or something of that nature."

"What?" Mary asked, she looked confused.

"Yes, it's in my blood you could say," she explained. "I wrestled with it all night and I keep coming back to that."

"Why can't you do that here?" Mary asked.

"I need a fresh start," Sarina said.

Mary nodded. "I see"—she fidgeted—"I hate to bring this up but what will become of the acreage we lease?"

"Well"—Sarina put her arm around her neighbor—"you can either purchase the land or I will make a stipulation that the new owner has to continue to lease the land to you for the same amount. I will leave that choice up to you and your husband."

Mary nodded, but frowned. "Well, okay then. Let me know if you need help packing the house."

Sarina thanked her neighbor and the two women walked back toward the house. They didn't talk any more about Sarina selling her house, but she could tell Mary was concerned.

The dust in the attic overwhelmed Sarina as she surveyed the big open space. There wasn't much in the attic, just some Christmas decorations and a pile of empty boxes. She walked over to the boxes and picked one up. She blew dust off the top but not all of it. "Oh well," Sarina said, "I have to pack so will just have to deal with the dust."

Sarina gathered as many boxes as she could carry and went back downstairs to the living room. She grabbed a rag from the kitchen and cleaned the boxes as best as she could and decided to start in the living room. She would work her way through the house from there and keep the packed boxes in the living room, out of the way.

She sighed, realizing how big of a chore lay in front of her, then grabbed the closest knickknack, wrapped it in paper and placed in the box. *One down and so much more to go.* Letting out a sigh, Sarina dove into packing for the rest of the day.

After taping the latest box, Sarina looked around the room. The light had dimmed, and she noticed the time just as her stomach growled signaling it was time for dinner. She glanced across the sea of boxes and was happy for the progress she made. She picked up a bag of items she decided to donate and set it by the fireplace.

Memories danced through her mind, and she gazed at her surroundings. She missed her parents, but she knew she would not really miss this house. Sarina was a little sad that the farm's legacy would end with her, but it couldn't be helped. She couldn't stay where she didn't belong. A memory of the villa flashed into her mind and she left the room as though she were running from her memories.

The following day Sarina rose early to tackle her mother's craft and sewing room, which doubled as a guest bedroom. She decided to donate most of the items. It didn't make sense to keep most of them. She kept an old quilt and a picture of the farm, which had been taken long before she had been born. Everything else was in the "donate" or "throw away" piles.

It was almost noon when Sarina carried the last box from the guest room into the living room. She had already taken the throw away items to the curb and the donate items to her car. She stacked the box and heard a knock on the door. Sarina had not heard anyone pull in, so she looked out the window and was surprised to see a familiar truck in the driveway. It was her father's oldest friend, Bob. Sarina grinned and answered the door.

Bob smiled down on Sarina as she opened the door, but his smile faded when he glanced behind her and saw the stack of boxes in the living room. "So," he said, "it's true. You are selling and moving away."

Sarina took a step back. "Please come in. And yes I am."

Bob walked in and glanced around. "Oh, the memories of this place ..."

"Come, let's go sit in the kitchen. Want some lemonade?" Sarina asked.

Bob followed her into the kitchen. "I have to ask, is everything okay, Sarina?"

Sarina tried to hide her surprise at the question while she gathered glasses. "Yes, why do you think things are not okay?"

"Well, you run off to Italy, come back and abruptly put your farm on the market," Bob explained. "It seems a bit odd."

"It took me going to Italy to finally realize something I always knew but didn't want to admit," she said. "I don't belong here, so it's time to go."

"Fair enough," Bob said. "Well, I came to give you an offer. Our land backs up to yours and it only makes sense for me to buy it."

Sarina's hand jerked and some of the yellow liquid sloshed over the rim of the glass. "Really?"

"Yes, really," Bob said. "And I will pay full asking price. I will even keep your house here. I plan to rent it out since it is in good condition."

"Oh," Sarina said. "I have one stipulation."

"What's that?" he asked.

"You continue to lease twenty acres to my neighbors Rick and Mary for the same amount as our contracted price," Sarina said. "It's a stipulation that I will not negotiate on or I won't sell it to you."

"Just like your father." Bob chuckled. "You have a deal."

Sarina beamed and handed Bob his glass.

Bob took a sip and stared at the lemony liquid. "It is no surprise that I love this land. And I promise I will take care of it in your father's name."

"Thank you," Sarina said. She knew that although she wouldn't be continuing the farm's legacy herself, Bob would, and her father would be happy with the arrangement. She lifted her glass and said, "Salute." Her eyes grew wide at the word that had slipped out of her mouth and looked over at Bob who seemed to be studying her.

"You sure you're okay?" he asked.

"I will be," she said.

"Okay. I will have my lawyer draw up the contract," Bob said. "And Sarina, don't forget we are here for you same as before. And just because you're leaving doesn't mean that changes."

Sarina walked over and hugged him. He chuckled, stood, and said he would be in touch. Sarina watched

him leave and felt happy. Things were coming together for her to leave, she just needed to figure out
where she was going to go.

The morning dawned with rain hitting against the
windowpane of Sarina's room. She opened her eyes
and spied the few empty boxes prepped and waiting
to be filled. She sat up, yawned, and frowned at the
daunting task waiting for her.

It was four weeks to the day since Sarina had arrived back from Italy and she had not heard from
anyone, not even Gigi. Sarina's frown deepened at the
direction of her thoughts and she wondered if her life
at the villa had been a dream. But the pain in her heart
reminded her it had been real.

Sarina rubbed her arm where the burn had healed,
and she couldn't stop the flood of memories that
rushed over her. She wondered what her Giacoletti
family were doing in that moment and she felt the
moisture spring in her eyes. She felt hurt, bruised,
tired, and sad, so she laid back down. She pulled her
covers over her head and cried herself back to sleep.

Two hours later, Sarina woke with a raging headache. She made jerky movements while she climbed
out of bed. She took a long hot shower, thankful it
helped ease her headache. Sarina went through the

motions of getting ready for the day, but decided she deserved a day of rest. Everything was packed except her mother's room and a few last-minute items. She was leaving her mother's room until last because she didn't want to deal with the flood of memories and the heartache, so she kept putting it off.

Sarina watched TV, read a few magazines, made chocolate chip cookies, and sat in silence on her covered porch watching the rain fall. She kept thinking of things that haunted her dreams and thoughts. When it was time for dinner, she felt depressed and lost and decided to go to bed early. She was on her way upstairs when she heard someone knock on her door.

A feeling of hope soared through her, and she wondered if it could be someone from Vetualini. But her smile faded when she answered the door.

"Well, that's a greeting from an old friend," Mary said.

"I'm sorry I guess I was hoping ..."

"Hoping I was someone from Italy perhaps?" Mary said.

Sarina shrugged and stepped back to allow her neighbor in.

Mary looked around and was amazed at all Sarina had accomplished in the last month. "So, you are all packed then?"

"Almost," Sarina said. "I just have Mama's room. I can't seem to bring myself to do it yet."

Mary's lips curved up, but she seemed sad. "Would you like some help?"

"No," Sarina said. "But thank you. It is something I must do on my own, but I will let you help me eat some chocolate chip cookies."

Sarina and Mary laughed as they walked into the bare kitchen. Sarina grabbed the plate of cookies, while Mary sat at the table.

"This seems so odd," Mary said.

"I feel the same way," Sarina said. She brought the cookies over to the table with two glasses of milk and set them down. "I know I am doing the right thing, but I still feel a little lost. Does that make sense?"

Mary nodded and asked, "When was the last time you didn't feel lost?"

Sarina frowned, played with her cookie, and whispered, "When I was at the villa."

"Then maybe that is where you are supposed to be," Mary said.

"No, not with everything that happened," Sarina said.

"Are you going to share what happened with me?" Mary asked. "I would so love to help."

Sarina let her tears rush out and the sobs shook her shoulders. Mary rushed to her and held Sarina until her cries diminished into a whisper of a sigh.

Mary pulled away gently. "Now what is this all about?"

Sarina didn't hold anything back when she shared her story with Mary. She explained about the keepsake box, her trip to Italy, her cousins, her grandparents, the villa, her mother's secret and how she'd uncovered the truth. Sarina shared about the fire, Alfonso's theft, and finally Antonio. Mary seemed entranced by the story.

"Love and loss are such a painful part of life," Mary said. "And to learn such things so young is heartbreaking, but you are strong, Sarina, and I know you will be okay."

Sarina sat back in her chair and took a deep breath. She had kept everything in for so long that sharing it now left her winded and tired. She stared out the kitchen window until she felt the squeeze of Mary's hand.

"You will be okay, Sarina," Mary repeated. "You are a strong brave woman with many talents to share. No matter where you go or what you do, you will be successful. I know this. And your hurts and pain will heal"—she paused—"I have to ask though. I heard you say only a few of your family members accused you or was it only one. Did no one jump to your defense?"

Sarina looked over at Mary. "I don't know. I was so hurt by what I heard, I didn't stick around to find out. I focused on clearing my name and left."

Mary smiled reassuringly and asked, "Could it be that you were in shock from what happened with Marco, you were fearful of the future at the villa and Antonio, and the pain from what felt like a betrayal was so overwhelming that you felt you had to leave?"

"I hadn't thought of it that way," Sarina said. "I wonder if I should have waited."

Sarina didn't share any more, but wondered if she had been wrong to leave the way she did. She took a final swig of her milk and tidied the milk and cookies snack. Mary talked with her about other things for a few more minutes, dismissed herself, and left. But not before promising to come by the next day to bring dinner.

Sarina watched her neighbor leave and wondered at Mary's questions.

Chapter Twenty-Three

The door swung open and rested against the door stop. Sarina took a deep breath and switched on the light. She looked around the room and forced herself not to cry. She knew she had to do this. It was necessary, but boy was it painful. Sarina could feel her mother's presence in the room, and it made her long for her more than ever.

Sarina backed from her mother's room and walked into the kitchen. She poured herself a cold glass of water, gulped it down, refilled the glass, and gulped down its contents a second time. She placed the glass in the sink and looked out the kitchen window at the sunny day. The leaves on the trees were changing colors and the air was cool now, but the sun made it look like it was warmer than it was. Sarina shivered, forced herself to turn away from the kitchen sink.

"Stop being such a ninny," Sarina whispered, took a deep breath, and walked back to her mother's room to get to work. She'd moved around the room for about an hour when she decided to work on her mother's dresser. Sarina was going to donate most of her clothes and was placing clothing in a bag.

Sarina pulled out an old sweater her mother always wore when she was chilled. It was faded and had a few small runs in it, but it was thick and warm. Sarina held it to her nose and breathed deep. She breathed in the scent of her mother—honeysuckle and soap. She placed the sweater in the keep pile and moved on to the next item.

As she pulled the last item out of the drawer, an envelope fell to the floor. Sarina picked it up and turned it over. The words were faded, the envelope was frayed, and it was addressed to her mother. She glanced around, as though checking to make sure no one else was there, even though she knew she was alone. She dropped the piece of clothing, crossed the room, and sat in a small chair next to the window. Her hands shook, which made it difficult for her to pull the worn letter out of the envelope. She unfolded the letter, took a deep breath, and read it.

> My Dearest Luc,
> It saddens my heart that you left your home under such awful circumstances, but you know that I have always believed that things happen for a

reason and that this perhaps is your destiny. You know that the villa is your birthright, but it will keep until you or your first-born returns home. I always believed that your future was here, but I now believe I was wrong in this. Your future is where you are now, in America. But I know in my heart that you or a part of you in your child will return and claim your birthright.

I write this to you because we had words before you left. I hope you know it was only because I wanted you to stay and claim what is yours, but you knew better than I. You knew that it was not meant to be. And I am okay with this now, for I only want your happiness. I love you, my sweet granddaughter, and I always will.

So, I will wait and continue on day to day preparing for your return or the return of the rightful heir in your first born, whichever it may be. I will not ask you again to return to us, but I will ask that you keep an open heart for your first born. I am getting old and tired and there will come a day I will have to decide who to leave our heritage to and my hope is that it will go to the first born of the first born as it always has and then perhaps things will be as they should be here once more.

Until we meet again, my sweet Luc.

Gigi

Sarina stared at the letter and looked outside. If she had read this several months ago, Sarina would have been confused but she was not confused now. She ached. She ached because she felt like she failed her mother and her great-grandmother. *I have made a terrible mistake by leaving the family, and Antonio, the way I did.* She wondered why she had not heard from anyone in Vetualini. *Maybe it's because you hurt them too.*

The breeze picked up outside and Sarina watched the swirling leaves and let her mind wander. She forced her mind back to packing and went back to the drawer where she found the letter.

"Oh," Sarina said and picked up a worn manila envelope from its resting place at the bottom of the drawer. She pulled out the documents and trembled when she realized what it was. It was the deed to the villa and the entire estate, and it had her name printed on it. She looked closer and realized her name was listed after all the first-born Giacoletti. It said she was the next heir. There was one more piece of paper.

It was a list of ingredients, and she realized it was for her mother's wine. The wine the family had drank in her mother's honor the night she had pledged to solve her mother's mystery.

Sarina struggled to put the papers back into the envelope. She stared at it and threw it on the bed, away from her, as though it were poisonous. "Oh no," Sarina cried. She ran out of the room, out the door and across her backyard. She kept running until she felt like her lungs would burst from the sobs that were rushing out of her.

Sarina stopped running and dropped to her knees. She buried her head in her hands and cried until she could cry no more. At one point she had sunk her entire body onto the grass and was staring up at the sky.

"I have made such a mess of things," Sarina said. "What am I going to do?"

The tears dried on her cheeks and she shivered from the chill in the air but didn't move.

"What am I supposed to do, Mama?" Sarina yelled.

A flash of memory of opening the keepsake box for the first time sprang into her mind and she thought back to when her mother had said, "This was my past, but it is your future.

Sarina sprung off the grass, ran back into the house, and up to her room. She looked around, expecting to find what she was looking for, but remembered she had left the keepsake box for Gigi at the villa. Sarina sat on the bed and wrapped her arms around herself.

It is time. For better or for worse, it is time to face things. Sarina felt a peace wash over her, and she knew what she had to do.

Sarina slowed a little when she saw the car but pedaled past it and stopped at her porch. She hopped off her bike and rested it against the porch. She turned just as a passenger door opened and a gray head peeked out from the top of the door.

"Oh," Sarina said and rushed to the car. "Gigi!

Sarina stopped short of her great-grandmother. *She doesn't look happy.* There was silence between them while Sarina mustered her courage. "What are you doing here, Gigi?"

"I could ask the same of you, my dear?" Gigi said.

Sarina's cheeks grew warm, but her pride made her stand her ground. "Perhaps I was mistaken, but I was not exactly wanted or trusted by—the family—so I decided to return here."

"I failed you, my sweet girl," Gigi said. "And for that I am sorry."

"You didn't fail me," Sarina said. "I failed to show you all that I was trustworthy, and I failed to do my part in the family. I flip flopped so much that I can't blame the family for not trusting me."

"The family trusts you, Sarina," Gigi said. "It is us that should have proven our trust to you."

"All this talk of trust and proving things," Sarina said. "It really doesn't matter to me somehow now. What matters is that you are here. And you came after me—but why did you come?"

"Because it was the right thing to do," Gigi said. "Especially after what you were led to believe in the end. We were all deceived and hurt by a family member who I will not name but he is no longer a threat or an issue." Her great-grandmother paused and shook her head. "He is about to face prison, and when he gets out, he will not be welcome at our home. And as for those that stood with him well, they are still part of the family, but are not welcome right now either. You must know though, most of the family didn't believe the lies, because they knew you. But I did fail, because I should have demanded to speak with you straight away instead of waiting. And for that I am sorry."

"Are you angry at me for leaving?" Sarina asked.

"No, Sarina." Gigi reached out and caressed Sarina's face. "I am angry at myself for allowing this to happen. I failed my Luc long ago and should have done things different to make it right. A mistake I should not have repeated. I am here to make things right."

Sarina rushed into her great-grandmother's arms and they both laughed.

"Please come inside," Sarina said as she pulled away. Sarina heard another car door open and another and her mouth dropped open. Nonna, her grandfather, Sofia and finally Antonio climbed out of the car. Sarina gasped, and ran toward her grandparents hugging each of them and Sofia. But she stopped short of Antonio. She was sure she had a guarded look, much as he did.

She studied him. Her thoughts raced while she tried to figure out what to say, but Antonio smiled his mischievous smile and said, "So you have not seen your handsome man in a month and all you can do is stare."

Sarina laughed and leapt into his waiting arms. The two hugged, kissed, and hugged again. They knew they needed to talk through some things, but for now it was enough to just hold each other.

"Come, please," Sarina said, "let's go into the house."

Sarina led the way and her family stopped short with mouths open wide when they saw the stacked boxes.

"What is this?" Gigi asked.

~ 318 ~

"I sold the farm and am moving," Sarina said feeling delighted.

"Where were you going?" Sofia asked.

"The villa for starters," Sarina said. "And from there—well—I wasn't sure."

Everyone started talking at once and Sarina chuckled. For the first time in a while, she felt genuinely happy, and a sense of belonging washed over her.

Chapter Twenty-Four

The wind blew Sarina's skirt and it brushed against her ankles while she stared out at the open sea. She stood on the dock in Vetualini, her mother's village, and now her own village. A month had passed since her family came to America to get her, and it had been a whirlwind of activity since.

Instead of putting her belongings in storage, Sarina's grandfather had paid to have it all shipped to the villa. And Sarina returned to the villa with Gigi, her grandparents, Sofia, and Antonio. Her eyebrows lifted, she felt her lips curl, and heat flushed through her body at the memory of her and Antonio making amends.

He has so much passion. I love him so much.

"Sarina, what are you doing, dear?" Gigi asked. "Are you coming aboard?"

"Yes," Sarina said. She smiled at her great-grandmother and climbed into the boat. She had decided to scatter her mother's ashes on the open water as it was the sea and the memory of it that had always brought her mother peace in life. It seemed right for her to be at peace there in death.

The vessel the family had chartered was not large enough to fit the entire Giacoletti family but there would be a family dinner at the villa later, in honor of Luc. The only ones on the boat were Sarina, her grandparents, her mother's siblings, Sofia, Antonio and his parents, and of course, Gigi.

The boat stopped at the designated spot Gigi had picked, and Sarina stood before the family holding her mother's urn close to her heart. Everyone waited for her to speak but she struggled to get the words out.

The wind blew across the deck of the boat and she felt a peace and happiness wash over her. She felt her mother give her strength. "My mother was a wonderful woman. She taught me everything I know about life and love."

Sarina paused and took another deep breath. "She was a beautiful woman inside and out. She was a quiet and meek woman when I knew her, but coming here, I discovered a whole other side to her. A vivacious, energetic woman who loved life and her family and the sea. She was a woman who was haunted by her past and a memory she hoped to regain to relieve her from the pain of it. It gives me great happiness to lay her to rest today having discovered the truth of her past. And I pray it has given her a peace in death that she longed to have in life. So, it is today that we scatter her ashes on the sea she loved, next to the village she loved, and her family she loved."

Sarina walked toward the side of the boat, reached into the urn, pulled out a handful of ashes and let them slip through her fingers into the clear blue water. "Rest in peace, Mama, I love you," Sarina whispered.

The rest of the family followed her example. Some whispered words of love, others brushed tears from their cheeks. When they were done, Sarina took the rest of the ashes and poured them into the sea. "The pain of the past is no more, Mama. You can now finally be at peace."

Antonio wrapped his arms around Sarina, and they sat together. They held each other as the boat turned and headed back toward shore.

Later that evening, the entire family gathered at the celebration of Luciana's life and Sarina's homecoming. Those who needed to make amends did and the night was a joyous occasion. At one point Sarina was filled with emotions from the joy and excitement of it all and she stepped away from the noise to catch her breath. She snuck into the shadows where she could watch at a distance.

She stood alone for a few minutes. When she heard footsteps, she looked over and saw Antonio walking toward her.

"You okay, my love?" he asked.

"Yes. I'm good. In fact, I'm great." Sarina said. "Just taking it all in."

He wrapped his arms around her and pulled her into a tender kiss.

"Promise me, you will marry me some day," Antonio said as they pulled apart.

"Oh!" Sarina said.

Antonio studied Sarina. "Are you about to tell me no?"

"Oh, no," Sarina said. "I was just thinking about what our future might be together. And yes, I promise I will marry you some day."

He pulled her into another kiss, but this one wasn't as tender. When the two came up for air they both turned toward the noise that was their family. They watched the chaos together.

"Come let's join them," Antonio said.

Sarina stopped him. "Yes, we will, but for a second or two I want it to just be the two of us and our promise to each other. Because you know how it will be once the family knows of our commitment to one another."

Antonio laughed and Sarina felt peace wash over her. It felt like a warm hug from her mother, but she knew it was much more than that.

"You know," she said. "I came all this way to find peace for my mother. But in that journey, I not only found peace for her, but I also found peace. A peace I didn't know I was searching for, and a place where I finally belong. The peace I found in my heart. And the belonging comes from my villa, my family, and you."

Antonio pulled Sarina into another kiss. It was a kiss of all the love they had for one another, and when they pulled apart, they walked hand in hand to their waiting family, and their future.

Acknowledgements

I want to thank all my family and friends who have supported me along the way. A special thank you goes to my husband, Rod, my daughter, Bri, and my three littles. You knew when I needed to work and willingly let me lock myself in my room or hide away somewhere so I could focus, and then jumped up and down with joy to help me celebrate every milestone of this process.

I would like to thank my parents, Galen and Paula, my brother Jeremiah, and my sister, Leah, who cheered me on. Special thanks to my little brother Josh who allowed me to pick his brain several times about his own adventures in Italy.

I especially want to thank my dear friend Andrea who believed in me without having read any part of my book. She helped me find the confidence to keep going anytime I faltered. Without her encouragement, I never would have started this journey to begin with.

And finally, there is one person whose help through this has been invaluable, my editor, Jeanne Felfe. Thank you for your faith in me and in my story, I couldn't have done this without you.

A Note to Readers

Thank you for reading *What Lies Across the Seas*.

If you enjoyed it, I would appreciate a review on your favorite retailer website.

And I'd love to hear from you. Drop me a line at esther@theestherschultz.com

My website is theestherschultz.com

About The Author

Esther Schultz lives by her personal motto of, "be kind always and spread joy every day." She believes everyone can live a peaceful, joy-filled life and attempts to spread that message in her work and daily life. Her favorite things include spending time in nature, especially along Lake Superior, and advocating for mental health. Esther lives in central Minnesota with her husband, four children, her dog, and horse.